"When have I d[...]
being smacked with[...]
asked, as he tried [...]
wet shirt that was clinging to his body.

"Only every time we're on the soccer field!" Shannon looked him straight in the eye.

His mouth fell open in disbelief. "You're upset about a little objective criticism? I've been trying to make you a better player."

He sounded so sincere that Shannon wasn't sure what to think. After all, he was the assistant coach. While she tried to sort things out, he reached over and lifted away a strand of hair that had stuck to her wet cheek.

"Now, you really owe me one," he said.

"Exactly what do *I* owe you?" she asked.

"How about tomorrow night?"

"Excuse me?"

"Come watch movies with me in the coaches' dorm living room," he said softly.

Shannon took a deep breath. She had to be crazy to accept an invitation from the guy who kept humiliating her on and off the field. But all she could think about was his handsome face and the way the sun made his blond hair look even blonder. Knowing it might be a mistake, she asked, "What time do they start?"

BANTAM SWEET DREAMS ROMANCES

PLAYING TO WIN
Janice Boies

BANTAM BOOKS
NEW YORK • TORONTO • LONDON • SYDNEY • AUCKLAND

RL 6, IL age 11 and up

PLAYING TO WIN
A Bantam Book / December 1990

ISBN 0-553-28078-3

Published simultaneously in the United States and Canada

Bantam Books are published by Bantam Books, a division of Bantam
Doubleday Dell Publishing Group, inc. Its trademark, consisting of the words
"Bantam Books" and the portrayal of a rooster, is Registered in U.S. Patent and
Trademark Office and in other countries. Marca Registrada, Bantam Books, Inc.,
666 Fifth Avenue, New York, New York 10103.

Printed in Great Britain by
BPCC Hazell Books
Aylesbury, Bucks

To the Eden Prairie Soccer Association

Chapter One

"Are you *sure* you'll be all right, honey?"

Shannon Nelson glanced at all the people in the Fire Lake Soccer Camp registration line. "I'll be fine, Mother."

"I'm just so sorry we can't stay to help you get settled into your room," her mother apologized.

Shannon didn't see many other parents sticking around to help their children unpack their suitcases. Sure, she had liked it when they had moved her into her cabin at sleepover camp in fifth grade, but she was sixteen years old now! "Don't worry about it, Mom. I know you and Dad have to get home for that wedding," Shannon said.

"Jake *is* my cousin's son. Everyone's expecting us," Mr. Nelson said, resting one hand on his wife's elbow.

Shannon's mother took a few steps toward the car. "You will write to us?" she asked.

"Of course." Her mother had only given her a month's supply of stationery and a book of stamps!

"In fact, why don't you call tonight?" Mrs. Nelson suggested.

Shannon looked over her shoulder at all the other kids. The two weeks at Fire Lake on her own were going to be great. "I don't know, Mom, I might be pretty busy . . . " she hedged.

"Just call collect so we know you're doing all right." Her father winked, pretending it was only Shannon's mother who was so concerned about her.

"Okay, I will." Shannon gave up trying to convince her parents she would be fine on her own. She hugged them goodbye, and then waited on the sidewalk, waving until the car was out of sight. It was nice to know they cared about her, but they had acted as though she was leaving home forever. Shannon shook her head. Parents. Who would ever figure them out? And it wasn't as if they were going to be alone in the house for two weeks. The entire town of Victoria, Michigan, would never be quiet as long as Shannon's younger sister April was around.

"Is this the end of the registration line?" Shannon asked a girl with wavy hair.

2

"Sure is." The girl wiped her brow. "I hope it's air-conditioned when we get inside. I've been standing here for fifteen minutes and I am *so* hot!"

Shannon laughed and lifted her long, dark-blond hair off the back of her neck. "I can't believe we decided to come to camp in August. We'll fry!"

"My mom and I were on vacation during the other sessions. We drove to Indiana to visit my grandmother," the girl explained.

"I was working," Shannon told her. "My parents said I had to earn half the money if I wanted to come here. So I spent the last two months waitressing at wonderful Benny's Family Restaurant."

The girl laughed. "At least we'll suffer together. My name is Lynda Larimer. I'm from Plymouth," she added, naming a suburb of Detroit.

"I'm Shannon Nelson, from Victoria."

"Is that far from here? I had to take the bus, and it took about four hours." She massaged her neck. "Only it seemed like eight!"

"I'm lucky. Victoria's only an hour away. My parents dropped me off." Shannon stood on her toes to get a better idea of how many people were in line ahead of her. "How many campers are supposed to be here?" she asked Lynda.

"I think a hundred girls."

Shannon scanned the crowd again. "So who are all these guys? We can't be the only two girls who didn't have boyfriends bring them to camp."

A boy behind Shannon cleared his throat. "There's a boys' camp here, too," he said.

Shannon looked over her shoulder . . . and up. The guy behind her was very tall, and he had a nice smile. "Really?" She shrugged. "I guess I missed that on the application." How could she have missed something as important as the fact that Fire Lake was a co-ed soccer camp? she wondered.

"We're not going to play against the guys, are we?" Lynda sounded worried.

"No, we have separate practices. But we do share a dining room," the boy informed them.

"Great," Lynda grumbled. When the guy stared at her, she explained, "I have the most obnoxious little brother. I was looking forward to two weeks without seeing anyone attempt to eat a whole cheeseburger in one bite."

Shannon couldn't help giggling. Although she didn't have a brother, her best friend Cindy back in Victoria had a thirteen-year-old one who loved to chug an entire can of cola without taking a single breath.

4

"Well," the boy began, "I can't speak for the other guys, but I promise to be on my best behavior in the dining hall. I'm—"

"Hey, Brent!" someone called from the registration desk.

"Well, now you know *my* name." Brent grinned and waved to his friend. "Gregg! How are you?"

Shannon followed Brent's gaze to a guy wearing a baseball cap. He looked slightly familiar. She watched him take off the cap and brush blond hair off his forehead. Then he smiled at Brent, and she saw the little space between his otherwise perfect front teeth. She had seen his picture in the *Victoria Herald* many times. What was *he* doing here? She turned to Brent. "You know Gregg Warner?"

"Sure. We were both in camp last year." He glanced at her with interest. "How do you know him?"

"We're from the same town."

"You go to the same school?" Brent concluded.

"No. I'm a sub for Hamilton High's varsity team and he's at Jefferson, but anyone who plays soccer in Victoria or even reads the sports page knows about Gregg Warner."

Brent nodded. "Yeah. He's pretty amazing.

That's why I'm a camper this year and he's a coach."

Gregg Warner was one of the coaches? Shannon hoped he was working for the girls' camp. It would be such a waste to put him with the guys.

Gregg wasn't just a star soccer player, he was the *cutest* soccer player in all of Victoria—and there were a lot of them. Shannon had come to Fire Lake to work on her skills so she could win a starting position on Hamilton's team at next month's tryouts . . . but camp had just taken on a new, more exciting dimension.

"*Who* are you talking about?" Lynda asked.

Brent pointed at the desk. "The blond guy wearing a Fire Lake T-shirt and a Detroit Tigers cap."

Lynda took a long, hard look at Gregg. Then she leaned closer to Shannon and whispered, "You know *him*?"

Shannon glanced up at Brent, not thrilled to think one of Gregg's buddies was overhearing their conversation. But he had run into another old buddy, and the two of them were busy reminiscing about what they had done at camp the previous summer.

Still, Shannon wanted to keep her voice low. "I don't exactly know him. It's more like I know *about* him," she said softly.

6

"Then this is your big chance." When Lynda grinned, her blue eyes sparkled. "Go over and introduce yourself."

"Introduce myself?" Last spring, Shannon had barely been able to stand up in front of her English class for an oral report because Bobby Matthews was in the room. Gorgeous guys made her tongue-tied.

"Sure. If he's been up here at camp since June, I bet he'd like to see someone from back home," Lynda encouraged her.

"I guess I could introduce myself as a fellow 'Victorian' . . ." Shannon mused. She watched him for a minute or two as he signed people in and gave them their dorm assignments. Her heart started hammering when she tried to imagine herself walking up to him. On the other hand, getting to know Gregg Warner might be well worth the risk. She took a deep breath, almost ready to make her move, when suddenly a tall girl with long, light-brown hair made her way to the front of the line where Gregg was working. "Forget it," Shannon mumbled as the girl struck up a conversation with Gregg.

"What?" Lynda squinted at the girl. "Don't let her stop you."

"You don't know her," Shannon said, trying to tell herself she was silly to be disappointed.

Gregg Warner would never have been impressed with her. In fact, she had probably just been saved from making a complete idiot of herself. "That's Deb Smith—she's a forward on my high school team. I can't compete with her," she told Lynda.

"Do you mean that she's a really good soccer player?" Lynda asked, confused.

"I mean she's the team's best forward . . . and she was president of the sophomore class . . . and she's on the honor roll every semester. *And* she's cute. You get the picture."

Lynda groaned. "Why are some people so perfect?"

Shannon shook her head. "I don't know."

"I guess you don't like her?" Lynda asked with a grin.

Shannon frowned. "It's not that I dislike her. I mean, she's really popular at school and all. But somehow we've never managed to be friends, on or off the field. We rub each other the wrong way, I guess."

"That can happen," Lynda said sympathetically.

"I just can't believe she's here!" Shannon cried. "Of all the sessions at all the soccer camps in this state, Deb Smith and I end up at the same one!"

*   *   *

"Can you believe we're roommates?" Lynda asked for the fifth time when they both threw their suitcases on the bottom bunk in room 353 of Jewell Hall.

"I'm glad," Shannon said. She had been a little worried about living with a stranger, but after spending thirty-five minutes in line with Lynda, they were getting along great. "Who gets the bottom bunk?"

Lynda winced. "Could I have it? I'm afraid of heights."

"Really? Do you freak out or something?"

"Yeah." Lynda didn't elaborate.

Realizing her roommate was embarrassed, Shannon pulled her stuffed teddy bear out of her suitcase and tossed him on the top bunk. "Rosebud likes it up there, so I guess I'll be okay."

"Rosebud?" Lynda asked with a giggle as she started to unpack her clothes and put them into the built-in dresser.

"When she was new she had a little flower behind one ear." Shannon shook out one of the sheets that someone had left on the desk. "Do you mind if I stand on your bed so I can make mine?"

Both beds were made and Shannon's suitcase was almost empty when someone knocked at their door an hour or so later. "Come in!" Shannon called.

"Hi! I'm Trish!" the redhead announced the moment she poked her head around their door.

"I'm Shannon."

"And I'm Lynda."

Without asking, Trish walked into their room and sat down on the bed. She fluffed Lynda's pillow and leaned against it, making herself comfortable. "I wanted to welcome you to Fire Lake," she said.

"Are you our dorm counselor?" Lynda asked.

Trish got an enormous grin on her face. "That's a laugh! They wouldn't have me, I'm sure. I'm probably lucky they even let me come back here as a camper this year."

Shannon pulled out a desk chair and straddled it. "Why?"

Trish rolled her green eyes toward the ceiling. "I guess you might say I caused a little trouble last year. But I didn't come here to talk about me. . . ." She pulled a sheet of paper out of her shorts pocket. "Would you be interested in buying a list of local restaurants, complete with phone numbers for delivery to the dorm?"

"Why would we need that?" Lynda asked. "Didn't we already pay to eat in the dining room?"

Trish wrinkled her nose in disgust. "If you call *that* food. . . ."

"Trish! Where are you?" someone called in the hall.

"She's in here," Lynda volunteered.

A tall girl with short, dark hair threw the door wide open. "Trish DeVere, are you bothering these girls?"

"You could at least be polite and introduce yourself," Trish told the intruder calmly.

"Hi. You must be Shannon and Lynda. I'm Darla Jones, the counselor for this floor."

"And I'm out of here," Trish said before she slipped into the hallway.

Shannon grinned. "Is she always like that?" she asked the counselor.

Darla ran a hand through her short hair. "Trish isn't exactly dangerous, but you should be careful around her."

"Why? What could she do to us?" Lynda asked.

"Give you brownies baked with salt instead of sugar . . . convince you to help her raid the boys' dorm late at night . . . talk you into a sit-down strike on the soccer field if the coach won't break out the juice when you want it. Need I say more?" Darla asked, smiling.

"I get the idea," Lynda said. "She's the camp joker."

"I don't think she ever means to get anyone in trouble," Darla quickly added.

"Okay. We'll think twice about anything she tells us," Shannon promised.

"Good." Darla clapped her hands as if she'd just defused one potential disaster. "Are you girls ready for the meeting in the commons?"

"What meeting?"

Darla pointed to the camp schedule lying on Shannon's desk. "All the girls are supposed to be in the commons by three-thirty for a review of camp policies. You'll also be assigned to teams."

Shannon checked her bright blue plastic sports watch. "It's three-twenty. We'd better get going!"

Chapter Two

" . . . So, ladies, if you remember these few rules, you should have no problems here at Fire Lake," the camp director concluded close to four o'clock.

"He didn't mention anything about the guys," someone said behind Shannon and Lynda.

"No, he didn't," Lynda whispered to her roommate. "Of course, when he told us about the weekend social events, I assumed they would be *co-ed*."

An older girl who looked like a counselor walked to the front of the room. She whispered something to Director Brown, who then cleared his throat and said, "It appears I have overlooked mentioning that there is also a boys' soccer camp on this campus. Let me just remind you that your dorm counselors will be watching for any *inappropriate* behavior."

The girls giggled at the director's obvious discomfort. It was clear he preferred to discuss soccer rather than social behavior. Shannon guessed he didn't have any daughters. Her own father always had plenty to say about dates and curfews and things like that.

"And now I'd like Coach Reeder to explain about the camp tournament," Mr. Brown said.

Shannon sat up when the big man replaced Director Brown at the podium. She hadn't heard anything about a tournament.

"You girls will be divided into teams and will practice together. Throughout the two weeks you are here, you will also be playing tournament games. The camp championship will be determined on your last Saturday here," Coach Reeder told them.

Shannon noticed the competitive looks on the faces around her. She was not the only one in the room who wanted to be on the championship team.

"Before you rush off to get your team assignments, I'd like to introduce the rest of the staff." Coach Reeder began reading from a list, and the other coaches stood up in the front row as he called their names.

Shannon was interested to see a few college-age girls stand up when the assistant coaches were introduced. Lynda was trying to whisper something in her ear, but Shannon's attention stayed on the rows in the front of the auditorium.

When Coach Reeder ended his list with, "Last, but not least, is assistant coach Gregg Warner from Victoria," Lynda elbowed her in the side.

Gregg stood and turned to face the girls. He was close enough that Shannon could see his deep blue eyes. Next to her, Lynda sighed.

"You think he's cute, too?" Shannon asked her roommate.

"Cute? Try gorgeous," Lynda suggested. "He could hypnotize me with those eyes!"

Shannon fell back against her seat cushion. If there were a hundred girls at camp, then Gregg Warner was going to have a hundred admirers.

"That does it," Coach Reeder announced from the podium. He pointed toward the hallway. "Stop at the table out there to pick up your team assignments and tournament schedule. And remember, we expect to see all of you on the fields at eight-thirty tomorrow morning."

Over half the girls groaned. Shannon quickly

tried to calculate how early she would have to get up to be on the field in time. Would the boys be around during practice? She knew it shouldn't make any difference, but it did. If they would be sharing the fields with the male campers, she wouldn't dare show her face without mascara and just enough blush to look healthy.

"And we expect you to be ready to *work* at eight-thirty." Coach Reeder seemed to enjoy rubbing in the early starting time. "No half-asleep athletes, please."

"I'm not even human until nine o'clock," Lynda complained as they joined the crowd heading for the table in the hall.

"When does your school start?" Shannon asked. "My first class always starts at eight o'clock, so I'm used to getting up early. Plus this summer I had the breakfast shift at Benny's, so I've been setting the alarm for five all summer."

"That sounds horrible! School starts at eight-fifteen for me," Lynda explained. "But fortunately, last year I had study hall first period. And this summer . . . well, let's just say that if I'm up by ten, I'm lucky."

"I'll splash cold water on your face tomorrow morning if you want me to," Shannon said.

Lynda giggled. "You might have to!"

"Can you believe we're on the same team?" Shannon asked Lynda while she checked her closet for something to wear. "I was so amazed when both of our names were listed under *Team Mexico.* It's almost like fate."

"I hope I'm good enough to be the starting goalie," Lynda said.

"I'm sure you are," Shannon mumbled, concentrating more on her clothes than on her roommate's worries.

"How would you know?" Lynda asked. "You've never even seen me play. Hey, what are you looking for, anyway?"

"Something to wear to dinner," Shannon answered.

"Why? Are we supposed to dress up?"

Shannon pulled her head out of the closet. "Well, no. I was just remembering that all the guys will be in the dining room and I'd like to look good."

Lynda hopped off her bed. "You're right. My cut-offs aren't going to impress anyone." She started rummaging through a dresser drawer.

They weren't the only two girls with guys on their mind when they tried to put on their makeup in the community bathroom down the hall. There was a girl at every mirror. Shannon brushed her long curly hair until it shone. Then she squeezed up to a mirror so she could add mascara to her thick, dark lashes and smudge a little peach eyeshadow on her eyelids.

"Who are you trying to impress?"

Shannon looked up, although she didn't need to look in the mirror to know that Deb Smith was standing behind her. No one sounded quite as mean as Deb when she was criticizing someone.

"You never know who you might run into," Shannon answered, determined not to let Deb get to her.

"Well, I suppose some people have to work hard to improve their chances," Deb said, fastening a barrette with a bow on it in her long, thick brown hair.

"Ohhhh . . ." Lynda growled at Deb's back as she strutted out of the bathroom. "She's vicious."

"My friend Cindy and I always tell ourselves she's trying to cover up how insecure she really feels."

Lynda squinted at Shannon. "Do you believe that?"

Shannon laughed. "Not for a minute. But we have to do something to make ourselves feel better."

Things didn't improve much at the dining hall. "How could they do this to us? I hate having a guy watch me eat chicken!" Shannon complained.

"Me, too." Lynda stabbed her chicken breast with her fork. "It will take me hours to eat this if I can't pick it up in my hands."

"The boys have it easy," the girl across the table told them. She nodded at the guys at the next table, who were picking up their chicken in their hands without giving it a second thought. "No one cares if they get grease on their chins. They don't have to act dainty and delicate."

"That's not fair," a girl named Franny Stern complained. She lived across the hall from Shannon and Lynda at the dorm.

"But it's so true," Lynda said with a sigh. "I've got a brother, and you should see him eat." She reconsidered and added, "Actually, you shouldn't. It's not a pretty sight."

The group at the table laughed. Shannon pointed out a gorgeous guy wiping his chin. "Would you turn down a date with him just because you didn't like the way he ate chicken?"

Lynda patted her chest to show how hard her heart was pounding. "Only if I were dead."

Franny chuckled in agreement. "Isn't it crazy? We spend half our time complaining about them and the other half—"

"Being miserable because they don't notice us," the girl across the table finished for her.

"I'm not sure about that," Lynda whispered to Shannon. "Look over there."

She followed her roommate's gaze and found Brent waving at them from halfway across the room. Shannon flashed him a happy smile. It was nice to know that he remembered them from the registration line. She noticed another guy approaching their table, but she didn't pay much attention until he sank into the empty seat across from Lynda.

"Hi, I'm Bart," he introduced himself in a nasal voice.

"Hi." Lynda couldn't have sounded less friendly if she'd tried.

Since he seemed to be interested in her roommate, Shannon took a good look at him. Bart was tall, but very thin. She could tell he was trying to make it look like his hair was spiked in front, but Shannon could recognize a problem cowlick when she saw one. Poor Bart. She hoped he played soccer well, because he wasn't going to break any girl's heart with his first impression.

Shannon let her gaze drift until she found

Gregg Warner . . . and Deb Smith. She inched forward on her seat to study them. Deb was leaning on the end of Gregg's table and Shannon couldn't help thinking she looked like a vulture hanging over his plate.

Did I really see Gregg slide a few inches to his right to get away from her? Shannon thought she must have imagined it. Deb's techniques had never impressed her, but they always seemed to work on guys.

Deb flipped her long hair over her shoulder in a smooth move that Shannon actually envied—until she watched Gregg pull a hair out of his mashed potatoes. Shannon covered her mouth, trying in vain to hide her laughter.

"Thanks a lot," Lynda said in a low voice just before she kicked Shannon in the ankle.

Shannon glanced at Bart, who didn't seem to have noticed anything—except Lynda. Through clenched teeth, she whispered, "I wasn't laughing at you. It's Deb and Gregg."

They both glanced across the room just as Deb plucked a carrot stick off Gregg's plate. Shannon wished he would snatch it back from her, but instead, he said something to Deb that made her giggle before she took a delicate bite. They chatted for a minute or two, and then Deb moved away from the table.

Shannon looked away as Deb headed in her direction, still munching on the carrot stick. She knew it was silly, but Shannon couldn't stop thinking that Deb was ruining her chances with Gregg. As if she had a chance with a guy like him!

"Hey, Shannon," Deb said, pausing at their table.

She tried to be casual when she said, "Oh, hi, Deb."

"What team got you?" Deb inquired.

Shannon ignored the sarcasm. "Mexico."

Deb's eyes widened a bit. "Really. I'm on Denmark. We play you tomorrow morning."

What a wonderful way to start camp, Shannon said to herself.

"What's wrong? Don't you think you'll be ready for us?" Deb asked with a smile.

Shannon shrugged. Until the team got together in the morning, she had no idea how good—or bad—they might be.

"Oh, we'll be ready, all right. I'm the goalie," Lynda said firmly.

"And I'm a forward." Deb paused. "We'll see who's better tomorrow." She strode across the cafeteria and sat at a table with a group of older players.

Lynda rolled her eyes at Shannon once Deb was out of sight. "That is one unfriendly person."

22

"She's not always quite that rude," Shannon told the group at her table, attempting to defend her Hamilton High teammate at least a little bit. "Everyone at school knows Deb always says what she feels."

"Well, she's wrong," Lynda said with an assurance that surprised Shannon. "Denmark won't beat us tomorrow."

"Or us," the girl across the table declared. "I'm on the Italy team, and we'll be sure to play our best against Denmark."

The table grew quiet as the girls thought about their teams and the two weeks ahead of them. Everyone looked up when Bart coughed. "So, uh, Lynda. Want to go into town with me tonight?" he asked.

Lynda just stared at him. At the other end of the table, some of the girls struggled to hide their grins.

"We could get a soda or something," Bart added when Lynda didn't jump at the chance to spend the evening with him.

"Uh, we have to finish unpacking tonight," Shannon said when she realized Lynda was speechless. If someone didn't help her roommate, she was going to end up on a date with a guy who was about as exciting as the cafeteria food.

"Yeah," Lynda agreed, finally finding her voice. "Our room's a mess."

"Tomorrow night, then?" Bart sounded hopeful.

Lynda shook her head. "I'll be dead after the first day of practice."

"We all will be," Shannon added. "It's supposed to be ninety degrees tomorrow."

"We could catch a movie on Tuesday," Bart persisted.

Lynda glanced at Shannon, her eyes saying she was out of excuses.

"Hey, didn't your parents say they would call you sometime Tuesday night?" Shannon improvised.

"Or afternoon," Lynda said quickly. "I don't know when they'll call. I'll have to stick around the dorm."

Bart seemed to get the message that Lynda was not dying to go out with him. Slowly he got up from his seat. "Well, I'm not sure about my schedule after Tuesday. But I'll see you around."

Lynda forced a bright smile. "Sorry, but thanks for asking."

She covered her face with her hands after he left. "Why me?"

"But did you notice?" the girl next to Shannon asked. "There wasn't a hint of chicken grease on his chin."

"Of course not," the girl across the table

24

replied. "He was probably the only guy in the whole dining room who ate his chicken with a fork and knife!"

Shannon couldn't help laughing. "Aren't we terrible? We complained about the guys who used their hands and now we're laughing at Bart because he was the only guy here with good manners."

"You know what?" Lynda let her hands slide away from her face. "It's pretty hard being a girl . . . but it just might be worse being a guy."

Dinner rolls flew in her direction as everyone cried, "No way!"

Chapter Three

"Go Mexico!" The girls clapped and backed out of their team huddle.

"Okay, ladies. Get out there and show me your best. I want to see what you can do!"

"All right, Coach." Trish DeVere actually winked at the big man on her way onto the field.

"We can do it," Lynda told Shannon as both girls watched Deb Smith strut onto the field. Of course, Shannon thought, Deb had already managed to convince her coach that she could play center.

"I guess we can beat her," Shannon said without conviction. In her light blue team shirt, Deb looked taller and tougher than anyone on the Mexico team.

"Between the two of us, she won't score a

single goal!" Lynda boasted as she took her position as goalie.

Shannon tried to concentrate on her full-back position on Lynda's right. To keep from fidgeting, she retied her shoelaces and checked to see that her yellow shirt was tucked into her shorts. Talking about Deb made her nervous. It was one thing playing on the same team with her at Hamilton, but Shannon wasn't looking forward to being on the opposing team.

"Pssstt . . . Shannon!" Lynda made it sound urgent.

She looked over her left shoulder and saw Lynda discreetly gesturing to the center of the field with her head. Had Deb fainted or something? Shannon wondered. She followed Lynda's direction, and smiled.

Gregg Warner was on the field, and Shannon wasn't the only girl noticing how cute he looked in his black shorts and white polo shirt bearing the Fire Lake logo. The late-morning sun made his sandy blond hair look lighter than it had in the cafeteria the night before. It also glinted off something metal on his chest.

"Are you staring at the ref?" Trish inquired with a chuckle from her fullback's position on the other side of the field.

"Ref?" Shannon then realized that the sun was shining off a referee's whistle—not a gold chain.

"Yeah." Trish pointed at Gregg as he talked to the center forwards for both teams. "Gregg Warner."

Shannon bit her lip. She didn't think Trish needed to know she thought Gregg was the most interesting part of the scenery at Fire Lake Soccer Camp. She shrugged noncommitally.

"He is *so* cute," Trish said enthusiastically. "I tried to get to know him last summer when he was still a camper . . . but I guess he doesn't like practical jokes." She shook her head. "It's too bad. He's a hunk."

"I hope he's a *fair* hunk," Lynda observed from behind them.

Trish and Shannon both turned and squinted at her. "What do you mean?" Trish asked.

"The center forward for Denmark has been putting the moves on him. I hope he can stay objective," she replied.

"If there's one thing I know about Gregg, he always plays fair," Trish said with the authority of an expert. Shannon hoped she was right.

It seemed as if only two seconds after the game started, Deb was racing down the field, heading straight for Mexico's goal. Shannon narrowed her eyes and tried to remember her Hamilton coach's advice: keep your eye on the ball, don't worry about how much the player is dancing around. But it was hard not to be impressed—and worried—by the smooth way Deb wove around the other players on her way to the goal. Shannon understood why other teams were so intimidated by her. She seemed unstoppable.

"Nelson, get ready!" Coach Reeder yelled from the sideline.

She blinked once and then the ball was right in front of her. Before Deb could try to kick it into the goal, Shannon pulled back her foot and booted the ball back across the center line.

"Good work!"

Shannon grinned at her coach. When she had found out she would be in Coach Reeder's group, she had been a little worried. After all, he had been the one who talked about the tournament at camp orientation as if he were the top coach or something. But he hadn't acted like an army general yet. Coach Piper back at Hamilton High was worse; every afternoon he put them through warm-up routines that would leave Jane Fonda breathless, and then sent them onto the field for an hour's scrimmage.

Shannon tried to keep her mind on the game while all the action was on the other end of the field, but it was hard to concentrate on soccer when Gregg was running back and forth across the field, looking gorgeous. When Gregg started trotting in her direction, Shannon realized one of the Denmark players was driving the ball toward her, too.

She was poised and ready when the ball angled past her . . . to Deb. How had she gotten behind Trish? Apparently, Gregg had the same question. It was illegal for anyone to get between them and the goalie unless they already had the ball.

His whistle shrieked. "Offsides on number nine!" he called loudly.

Deb glared at him when he gave the ball to Shannon's team. When everyone chased the ball back toward the far goal, Shannon looked over her shoulder to Lynda. "Still worried about the ref?" she asked.

"Only that he's too cute. How are we supposed to concentrate on the game?" Lynda complained.

"You, too?" Trish asked. She rubbed her chin and watched him carefully. "It's hard to believe, but he looks better now than he did last year . . . and last year he was pretty great."

"It's not like I have a crush on him," Lynda protested.

"Me either," Shannon observed, although she had a feeling Trish would believe whatever she wanted to. Shannon did think Gregg was the best-looking guy at camp, but she didn't expect to ever really talk to him.

"Come on, ref!" a familiar-sounding voice yelled.

Shannon snapped to attention. Deb was in front of Gregg, stamping her foot, and Shannon strained to hear what she was saying.

"You called me for offsides down there. So why didn't you call this—"

Deb pointed to Samantha Sullivan, one of Shannon's teammates, who was standing near the goal. Apparently Deb thought the girl had planted herself near the goal without any Denmark players around except the goalie, just waiting for someone to pass her the ball. It was a guaranteed way to score a goal, but totally unacceptable.

"I didn't call it because she wasn't offsides. Number seven was between her and the goal," Gregg maintained. He pointed to another Denmark player.

"When did you have your eyes checked last?" Deb demanded, and several girls from her team giggled. Gregg folded his arms over his chest while she continued. "Maybe you need glasses," she said.

"That's enough," he said, his voice ringing with authority. He pulled a yellow card from his pocket, showing everyone he was warning Deb to watch her sportsmanship.

"All right!" Lynda said under her breath.

Shannon gave her a thumbs-up sign as Gregg signaled for play to resume. An angry Deb soon had the ball under control again. She was heading right for Shannon until another member of the Mexico team tried to block her. Shannon couldn't see exactly what happened, but her teammate fell backward as Gregg's whistle blew again.

"Pushing on Denmark," he declared, staring at Deb.

Deb's hand flew to her chest. "Me?"

Gregg nodded. He looked as though he was expecting another argument.

Deb pressed her fingers against her forehead. "I know how to officiate a soccer game," she informed Gregg and everyone else on the field. "I referee a lot of games back home for the younger leagues, and I know good reffing when I see it."

Gregg raised his eyebrows. Shannon got the distinct impression he was waiting for Deb to hang herself. "What's your point?" he asked.

"You need to learn a few things!" she exclaimed.

32

The red card appeared from behind Gregg's back as if by magic. Shannon couldn't believe it. Gregg was kicking Deb out of the game! Of course, she deserved it, but Gregg had to be pretty sure of himself to kick a player out during the first quarter of the first game in the tournament.

Deb stomped off, kicking up a chunk of grass that landed on Gregg's shoe. She glared at him and he stared back at her. When he jerked his thumb toward the sideline, indicating that was where Deb belonged, Shannon couldn't help laughing.

After making sure Deb had gotten off the field, he looked directly at Shannon. She held her breath. Was he going to give her the yellow card for laughing?

He stared at her for a second, and then the corners of his mouth turned up in a half-smile, revealing the tiny gap between his front teeth. Before Shannon could force herself to look away, he winked at her, as if they'd both been in on a plan to kick Deb out of the game.

Shannon turned toward Lynda. "Did he just—"

"I know he wasn't winking at me," Trish said before Shannon could voice her full question.

"And he wasn't looking at me," Lynda said with a sparkle in her eyes.

"Nelson!" Coach Reeder hollered. "Look alive out there!"

Shannon snapped back to attention. The soccer ball was headed in her direction, and she scooted around two Denmark players to quickly boot the ball out of Mexico's territory. She couldn't help glancing at Gregg to see if he had noticed her technique, but he was already running back down the field, following the action.

"I am so hot," Shannon complained when the game was over. She pulled her hair out of its elastic and redid her ponytail so that all of her hair was off her face.

"I feel fine," Lynda said. "Of course, you were playing so hard that the ball never even came near the goal."

Shannon smiled. "I guess I did have a pretty good game."

"You mean you don't always play like someone possessed?" Lynda picked up a water bottle and squirted some liquid into her mouth.

"No, this is pretty normal for me. Average, I mean." She reached for Lynda's water bottle and squirted some of the lukewarm water down her throat.

"If you're average, then I'm a beginner, unless . . ." Lynda's eyebrows arched. "Were you by any chance working extra hard to impress the ref?"

"Gregg?" Shannon practically choked on the name.

"I think you need some more of this." Lynda offered her the water bottle with a grin.

Shannon shook her head as they continued to walk off the field. "It's been in the sun too long. But I'd absolutely kill for a chocolate malt."

"Did someone mention a malt?" a guy behind them inquired.

"She did," Lynda volunteered before either of them realized who was hurrying to catch up with them.

Shannon was stunned when Gregg Warner fell into step beside her. "Would you like to join me and some of my friends at Burger Heaven?"

"How are their malts?" Shannon asked. Then she wanted to kick herself. She didn't know which was harder to believe—that Gregg was talking to her, or that she had asked something as stupid as whether or not the malts were good. If it meant she could spend some time with Gregg Warner, she wouldn't care what the malts were like!

"They have great malts. I recommend the double chocolate," Gregg said.

Shannon smiled. "Sounds perfect."

"Then you'll come with me?" He looked from Shannon to Lynda and back again.

"We'd love to," Lynda answered quickly. "My name is Lynda Larimer."

"And I'm Shannon Nelson."

"Since we're getting personal, I'm Gregg Warner." His dark blue eyes sparkled as he smiled at each of them in turn.

"I know." Shannon smiled up at him, surprised that he was almost a head taller than she was.

He ran a hand through his short, damp hair. "You've got a good memory. Coach Reeder introduced all of us so quickly."

"No, I'm from Victoria," she explained, remembering how she and Lynda had joked about her introducing herself as a fellow Victorian during registration. "That's how I know you."

"Funny. I don't think I've seen you around." He frowned as if trying to remember her. "Who do you hang out with?"

"No one you know. I go to Hamilton."

"Ah." He nodded. "I go to Jefferson."

Shannon almost said *I know* a second time, but stopped before she could give Gregg the impression she knew his whole life story. Instead, she decided to play innocent. "Do you play soccer there?"

"I'm the starting goalie."

"I'm a goalie," Lynda put in.

"I know. I didn't get to see much of you today because Shannon didn't let the ball get near you." He grinned at Shannon and she smiled in return. Then he continued, "But I'm going to know a lot more about both of you. Coach Reeder just asked me to be his assistant coach."

Shannon wondered if she was dreaming. Or maybe she'd died and gone to heaven—real heaven, not Burger Heaven. What could be better than seeing Gregg Warner every single day for the next two weeks? It was starting to look as though all those early morning practices would be well worth it!

Chapter Four

"Don't I know you?" one of Gregg's friends asked when Lynda and Shannon slid into their big booth at Burger Heaven.

Lynda studied him for half a second, and then snapped her fingers. "The registration line."

"That's right. We were suffering together yesterday while certain . . ." He paused to look at Gregg. "While certain people had the advantage of sitting in the shade."

Gregg laughed. "I ran inside to the air-conditioned lobby whenever I got a break."

"So can we get some proper introductions?" the second guy asked.

"Of course," Gregg agreed, glancing at Shannon and Lynda. "You both seem to know my friend Brent Parks. The girl next to him is Susie McReynolds and that guy is Joe Morris."

Shannon murmured a quick hello to everybody, but her concentration failed her as she thought how amazing it was to be sitting next to Gregg. Lynda was on the other side of him. If her roommate hadn't been there, too, Shannon would have thought it was all a dream.

He tapped Lynda on the shoulder. "This is Lynda Larimer, the girl who won't let anyone score."

Everyone burst out laughing, except for Lynda, who blushed furiously.

"We could use you on my team, Lynda," Susie said when the laughter died down. "Seriously."

"I bet you could use Shannon, too," Gregg said with a smile that made her heart skip a beat. "She's super at fullback."

"When do I get my double chocolate malt?" Shannon asked, trying to change the subject as she felt her cheeks turn pink, too.

"When do you want it?" the waitress asked.

Shannon's cheeks grew hotter. She hadn't seen the waitress coming up to the table, and she knew she must have sounded incredibly rude.

"I think she needs it immediately. You know how hard it can be dealing with a malt addiction," Gregg said, patting her on the shoulder.

As he gave the waitress their order, Shannon was grateful that he had covered for her, but she was more aware of his touch. Her skin seemed to be burning beneath her shirt. Gregg must have read her mind; he moved his hand to the table and started fiddling with a napkin.

"Is this your first year at camp?" Susie asked.

"Yes," both Lynda and Shannon answered.

"Where are you staying?" Joe wanted to know.

"Jewell Hall," Lynda said. "We're roommates."

"You're in Trish's dorm." Susie's big brown eyes twinkled. "Watch out for her."

"We've already been warned." Shannon let her gaze shift to Gregg. After what Trish had said about bombing out with him, she wondered how he felt about her. He seemed amused by the mention of her name, just like the others.

"Sometimes I wish I could be as wild as her," Susie admitted.

"No, you don't." Gregg sounded quite definite. "One Trish in camp is enough. Besides, I can't imagine you sneaking into the boys' dorm to write love poems all over the bathroom mirrors with lipstick."

Brent burst out laughing. "I'd forgotten about that," he said, catching his breath. "When I stared into the bathroom mirror, half-asleep, my face looked all red. I thought I had some horrible disease!"

"Don't you always look that bad in the morning?" Gregg teased.

Susie shook her head. "Why did she do it? I never heard who her intended victim was."

Gregg shrugged his shoulders. "No one ever knew. She wrote things about half the guys in the dorm. If she had one person in mind, we couldn't tell who it was."

Shannon wondered if that had happened before or after Trish realized Gregg didn't like practical jokers. For a moment, Shannon thought about Gregg's having to put up with things like Trish's silly games and Deb's blatantly flirtatious moves. Maybe it was hard being a good-looking guy.

"If Trish tries to involve you in one of her plans, I think you should run the other way—"

"And fast!" Gregg finished for Susie. He sighed. "Hey, did you guys know Shannon is from my hometown, Victoria?"

"Do you go to the same school?" Joe asked.

"No," Gregg answered. "Poor Shannon goes to Hamilton."

"Excuuuse me." Shannon squared her

shoulders. "He only talks that way because he knows Hamilton is a much better school than Jefferson."

Lynda's mouth fell open. But Gregg didn't seem bothered in the least.

He grinned as he explained to the others. "You can probably tell we have a fierce cross-town rivalry. Hamilton is the new school. It's too bad someone forgot to tell the people over there that newer—and trendier—doesn't always mean better."

Without thinking, Shannon nudged Gregg sharply in the ribs with her elbow.

"Hey, offsides!" he joked, his blue eyes dancing with amusement.

Everyone stared at them, trying to understand the private joke, and Shannon wanted to crawl under the table. It wasn't like her to do something so bold; it had just surprised her when Gregg ended his explanation with another zinger.

She was saved by the malts. The waitress came toward them with six tall glasses balanced on her tray.

"Two-to-one odds she drops them," Joe whispered.

"They never drop the trays here," Susie said. "Remember the time we each ordered three malts just to see if the waitress could handle the load?"

"That's mean!" Shannon said. "I was a waitress this summer and there's nothing more embarrassing than dropping someone's order."

"How would you know?" Brent asked.

"Well, early one morning—really early—I was bringing this regular customer, Mr. Patula, his three eggs, over easy. He ordered the same thing every morning. But that day, some lady left her purse next to her chair and I tripped over it."

"You didn't!" Lynda cried.

Shannon nodded. "I did."

The Burger Heaven waitress interrupted Shannon's confession when she safely delivered the malts with a smile. The kids were quiet while they took their first tastes, then Gregg grinned at Shannon. "You haven't finished your story."

Looking back, Shannon could smile at the memory, but it hadn't been very funny at the time. "Mr. Patula's plate flew into the air and flipped four times before the eggs, and then the plate, landed on his lap."

"No way!" Susie exclaimed. "What did he do?"

"He peeked under the plate and said, 'Don't worry, honey. I like scrambled eggs, too.' "

Gregg threw his head back and laughed. "Did that *really* happen?"

Shannon traced an X on her shirt. "Cross my heart. It's the truth."

Gregg looked at her and shook his head. "So which fine restaurant in town was lucky enough to have *you* this summer?"

"Benny's Family Restaurant," she told him.

He moved closer to her and whispered, "Who's Benny? I've always wanted to know."

She didn't dare turn to face him because their noses might bump. Softly, she said, "Promise not to tell?"

"I promise," he said solemnly.

"Benny is the owner's cocker spaniel."

Gregg leaned back against the cushion, chuckling and leaving the others to wonder for the second time what they had missed. Although Shannon loved feeling as if she and Gregg were sharing private jokes, the attention was making her uneasy.

Brent seemed to sense her discomfort and he changed the subject. "Uh, Gregg, what's been happening around camp this summer?" he asked.

"The first session went well." Gregg sat up and scooped some of the whipped cream off the top of his malt. "Nothing unusual happened until early July."

Joe nodded knowingly. "Firecrackers again?"

"Of course." Gregg shrugged, glancing at Susie. "It happens every year."

44

Susie threw a napkin across the table and barely missed the top of his malt. "You knew I was in on it?"

Shannon smiled at him as he began to laugh heartily. Gregg Warner was full of surprises. First, it had been a miracle that he had invited them to Burger Heaven with the older campers. Second, it had been easy to talk to him. And finally, the guy wasn't just great-looking, he was fun. The two weeks were going to go very fast if she got to spend much time with him.

"Have you seen *Perfectly Awful*?" Susie asked the group, naming one of the summer's hot movies.

"I've been stuck here at camp," Gregg complained as though being an assistant coach took up all of his time and required incredible sacrifices.

"But it just came to the theater in town," she told him. "I saw it on the marquee. You should see it; it's so funny."

"I love funny movies," Lynda said.

"Me, too." Shannon couldn't help looking up at Gregg. "I haven't seen *Perfectly Awful* yet either."

He nodded. She hoped he was filing that information for a future date.

"The popcorn is great at the theater here," Joe said.

"But Shannon likes malts," Gregg reminded him.

"Then you should find someone who'll take you to Mama's Kitchen," Susie suggested. "The malts are good here, but no one makes them like Mama."

"Where is this place?" she asked Gregg with a smile.

"Too far to walk," Susie answered for him. "You need a friend with a car."

Although Shannon had started feeling comfortable with Gregg, she didn't dare look at him. If she fluttered her eyelashes and asked if he had a car to take her to Mama's Kitchen sometime . . . Shannon sighed. She just couldn't do it. Some girls could be that bold, but she'd never learned the knack of flirting.

"Are you all right?" Gregg asked, looking at her with concern.

She stared at the little bit of chocolate stuck at the bottom of her glass. Her nervousness was obviously showing. "I'm fine," she assured him.

The group broke up a few minutes later, and Gregg walked the two girls back to Jewell Hall. When he paused on the bottom step in front of the dorm, Lynda said, "Thanks for inviting us. It was fun meeting your friends, and I *needed* that malt after our game."

46

"Yeah," Shannon began, finally finding her voice. "I had a good time."

"You're pretty fun too," he said, leaving Shannon to wonder if he was talking about Lynda, or her, or both of them.

Just in case he was speaking to her, Shannon smiled and said, "I think you're okay, too—for a Jefferson guy."

"Make all the Jefferson jokes you want to . . . today." His grin was positively wicked. "Just remember that tomorrow *I'll* be the one in charge."

He tried to make it sound like a threat, but Shannon couldn't think of anything better than working with Gregg in the morning. Feeling pretty confident, she looked him in the eye. "I won't forget."

His grin grew wider. "Neither will I."

"Shannon Nelson, would you please demonstrate dribbling through the cones?" Gregg called out the next morning.

Shannon nudged her soccer ball toward the first cone on the field, trying to keep her smile to herself. She had tried on three different shorts and tops that morning before she found the right combination. Her efforts had obviously been worth it; he had noticed her.

47

He was tapping one finger on his clipboard when she finished the drill. "Very good. What did you think?" he asked the rest of the Mexico squad.

"Could she go faster?" Samantha asked.

Gregg nodded. "Good point."

"She could go closer to the cones," Trish noted.

Shannon had felt bad enough at the first criticism, but now Trish was knocking her work . . . and Gregg was agreeing with her! She wished she could crawl under one of the pylons that looked like they belonged on a road construction site.

She tried to stay close to Lynda after Gregg finished picking apart her dribbling demonstration. He was making her sound like a failure for not being perfect on the second day of camp. *Keep your head up. Make sharper cuts around the cones. Go for speed.* What had happened to the nice, friendly guy she had sat next to at Burger Heaven yesterday?

She and Lynda both groaned when he announced it was time to practice headers. Shannon was willing to work hard, but there was something about bouncing balls off her forehead that scared her. She liked to say it was her desire for self-preservation that made her flinch half the time.

48

"Nelson, be aggressive!" he yelled across the circle.

She glared at him. It was easy for *him* to tell her to smack her head against the ball; he was standing safely in the center of the circle tossing the ball at one girl's head and then the next.

Gregg kept coming back to her until she finally did three good headers in a row. Shannon was beginning to think he was trying to restructure her face.

She gently rubbed her forehead as she and Lynda walked back to their dorm. "Why did I ever think Gregg Warner was nice?"

"He was just coaching us," Lynda observed.

"Maybe," Shannon said, "but even Sniper Piper doesn't harass me that much."

Lynda started to giggle as they passed the row of pine trees separating the soccer fields from the dorms. "Sniper Piper?"

"The coach at my school. Sometimes he's mean, but even *he* doesn't try to make me do things I just can't do." Shannon had never thought she'd defend Coach Piper, but after today, he seemed like a pushover in comparison.

"But you have to learn to do headers if you want to be a good soccer player," Lynda reasoned.

Shannon touched the spot on her forehead that she was convinced was turning black and blue. "This has nothing to do with my soccer career. Obviously things didn't go as well yesterday as I thought they did."

"You mean you think he was getting back at you for something you did at Burger Heaven?" Lynda's tone of voice made it clear she thought the idea was ridiculous.

"What if it was the Jefferson jokes? Maybe he doesn't like people cutting down his school," Shannon theorized.

"But he laughed just as hard as you did when he teased you about Hamilton," Lynda objected.

"Sure he did, but maybe he really didn't think the jokes were funny. Oh, who knows? Maybe I slurped my malt when I got to the bottom of my glass," Shannon worried as they walked up the three steps to the front door to Jewell Hall.

"You didn't slurp," Lynda assured her. "I was there. Trust me. You drank like a lady."

Shannon shook her head and sighed. "I guess it doesn't really make any difference what I did wrong. He doesn't like me, so I can give up hoping for a summer romance."

"Lighten up, Shannon! All he did was make a few comments about your soccer skills!"

"You can be honest with me. I know I'm not a great athlete, but even I'm not as bad as he made me sound."

Lynda opened the door to their room and collapsed on her bottom bunk. "He was pretty rough on all of us. I'm exhausted."

Shannon smiled. "It's nice of you to try and cheer me up. But let's face it. I was crazy to think Gregg Warner was interested in me. The only thing he cares about is Team Mexico winning the championship!"

51

Chapter Five

"Enjoying your last lunch?" Trish asked when she paused by Shannon's dining table Wednesday at noon.

"What's that supposed to mean?" Franny asked.

"I bet she heard one of those the-world-is-going-to-end-today predictions," Lynda scoffed.

"Laugh if you want to, but you'll know what I mean soon enough," Trish said mysteriously. As she flounced off to talk to another table of girls, she called over her shoulder, "It's Black Wednesday!"

"What's tomorrow? Purple Thursday?" Lynda joked, taking a pickle off her hamburger.

"Do you think Trish's brain waves would

be all over the chart on an EEG?" Franny asked.

"Not really," Shannon said. For some reason, she liked Trish. She admired her free spirit. "I think Trish is an individual."

"That's for sure," was the most agreement she could get from Lynda.

Team Mexico met on the practice field after lunch. Waiting for Coach Reeder and Gregg to arrive, Shannon idly twisted her curly hair between her fingers. She hadn't made any fuss about fixing it for the afternoon practice session. She hadn't even bothered to repair her slightly smudged makeup.

The coach and his assistant came onto the field together. "You girls are going to get a break this afternoon!" the coach announced.

Some of the girls cheered, but Shannon reserved her judgment. To him, a break could mean they would only have to run around the field twice instead of three times.

"Did any of you notice the camcorder this morning?" Coach Reeder inquired.

A few girls muttered that they had thought the guy with the camera was someone's father, but Shannon honestly hadn't noticed him. She had concentrated on keeping out of Gregg's way during the scrimmage, and her plan had worked quite well. He had only commented on her moves twice.

"Well, we're going back to the dining hall to view the films now. I hope you won't mind relaxing in the air-conditioning. Since all the teams are filmed, we'll have to wait our turn to see you on television."

"Make me a star," Trish joked as the girls walked back to the dining hall.

"What happened to your gloom-and-doom mood?" Lynda asked her.

Trish narrowed her eyes, giving her a look that indicated I-know-something-you-don't. "You'll see what I was talking about," she said.

Lynda looked at Franny and they both shook their heads. Shannon knew they were reconsidering the status of Trish's brain. She figured Trish was just trying to scare them because they were first-timers at the camp.

Shannon had just about reached the dining hall when she felt someone behind her tap her on the shoulder. She turned around.

"How's it going?" Deb Smith asked.

Shannon did a double take. She and Deb had never really made small talk. "Well, it's sure been hot," she said.

"You're not kidding." Deb pointed at her sunburned nose.

"Hey, Deb! Over here!"

The guy calling Deb was tall, with dark, curly hair. Shannon had seen him around the dining hall a few times.

"Sorry, Shannon. I gotta go." Shannon noticed that Deb didn't sound too sorry to break off the conversation, though.

When Shannon and her friends got into the dining room, it was already full. The long tables had been pushed against the back wall. Campers covered nearly every inch of floor between the tables and the television at the other end of the room.

"Do you see our team?" Lynda inquired.

Shannon stood on tiptoe and spotted Coach Reeder in the corner. "Over there."

They picked their way around the other teams that had already congregated on the floor. "Do you see any room for us?" Lynda asked once they located their team.

"Only if we hadn't eaten lunch," Franny joked. She pointed to a small spot on the floor.

While the other two girls jostled for a place on the floor, Shannon searched for another free space.

"Shannon!" Gregg called, to her utter surprise. "There's some room here."

Gregg was sitting on a window ledge and

he moved a little closer to the guy next to him, whom Shannon recognized as an assistant coach. Since he was going to the trouble to make space for her, she would look pretty rude if she ignored him. Besides, sitting down—even if it meant sitting by Mr. Congeniality—would be better than standing until their team's turn.

"How have you been?" he asked, as though he hadn't been criticizing and tormenting her for the past day and a half of practices.

She blinked and stared at him. It was hard to believe he actually cared. "I've been surviving."

"Merely surviving? Going away to camp is your big chance to live it up." He leaned back to take a good look at her. "Are you tired?"

Great. The first day she hadn't bothered to put on makeup, Gregg Warner decided to comment on her appearance. Wasn't it bad enough he found fault with her soccer skills at practice? Couldn't he leave her alone when she wasn't on the field?

"I know—you've been partying every night, haven't you?" Gregg concluded. "I hear Jewell is a pretty wild dorm."

"You're kidding, right?" At least on Shannon's floor, all the lights were out by ten o'clock. Everyone was too worn out from the long, hot practice sessions to do anything but sleep.

"Sorry—just a joke," he said, sounding concerned. "Are you sure you're all right?"

"Like I said, I'm surviving." Part of her wanted to be nicer to him, since he actually seemed a little worried about her, so she added, "Everything's fine."

"Have you been homesick?"

Shannon couldn't help laughing at the idea that she was wasting away from homesickness. "Would you miss a fourteen-year-old sister who practices the drums whenever you're on the phone?"

"Probably not." He smiled at her, and Shannon thought her heart would stop beating when she looked into his deep blue eyes. "I've got one brother. He's a junior at Michigan State University, in restaurant management. Whenever he comes home he tries out his most exotic recipes on the family."

"Is the food good?" Shannon asked.

He shrugged. "I've only had to have my stomach pumped once."

"Really?"

Gregg nodded. "Actually, it wasn't his fault the oysters were spoiled."

Shannon shuddered. The idea of eating oysters was almost as disgusting as the concept

57

of having her stomach pumped. "You must be brave," she observed.

"I like to think so." He puffed out his chest until the guy next to him whacked him on the back.

"Knock it off, Warner. You told me you almost fainted in the emergency room."

"Thanks a lot, Steve." There was a hint of a blush on Gregg's tanned face, and Shannon couldn't help but grin. He had put her in awkward positions often enough; it was only fair he had a turn.

"Who's your friend?" Steve asked.

"This is Shannon Nelson. She's from Victoria," Gregg said.

"I'm honored." Steve reached past Gregg to shake her hand. "According to Gregg, Victoria is the best town in all of Michigan. I'm Steve Brand, a poor guy from Grosse Pointe."

"That's too bad." Shannon shook her head, pretending to feel sorry for Steve. He only happened to live in one of the most exclusive areas of the whole state. "What do you do here?"

"I'm the assistant coach for Team Canada." He elbowed Gregg and asked in a low voice, "Why don't I have any girls who look like Shannon on my team?"

"What can I say?" Gregg asked with a

crooked grin. "You've got the money and I've got the luck!"

Shannon ignored the faint warnings in her head. They were trying to remind her how Gregg had destroyed her confidence during practice, but she refused to listen. Even if he and his friend were just teasing each other, Shannon was encouraged. She couldn't imagine any guy saying the things Gregg was saying unless he liked her, at least a little.

Laughter started at one end of the room and began to spread. Shannon looked over to the television screen in time to see a coach rewinding the tape. He replayed it in slow motion to explain how the ball had gotten past the goalie, and then he made a few humorous comments about the goalie's belly flop. It seemed like everyone except Shannon was laughing.

Shannon felt sorry for the girl. It would be horrible to have a whole roomful of campers laughing at her. On the other hand, she was relieved. No matter what mistakes she had made in front of Gregg, she had never looked as bad as the goalie on the tape.

"I'm up next," Steve announced when the other coach finished his review. As one team stood and stretched the kinks out of their legs, Steve's Canada team took their places in front of the television set.

"Have you had any good chocolate malts lately?" Gregg asked her after they had watched Steve's critiques for a while.

Shannon shook her head. "Not since Monday afternoon. Think you could convince the camp cooks to provide them at meals?"

"I doubt it," he told her with an easy grin. "I've been a camper here every summer since I was twelve. Last year was the first year they started serving edible food."

"Some people still don't think it's fit for human consumption," she said. It was so easy to talk to Gregg when he was making an effort to be nice. "My first day in the dorm, Trish tried to sell Lynda and me a list of restaurants that would deliver to the dorm."

Gregg's mouth fell open. "That girl's unbelievable! Steve and I put that list together three years ago. And now she's making money selling it?"

"I said she was *trying* to sell the list," Shannon explained. "I'm not sure she got any customers."

"You know, you're the only person here who doesn't make fun of Trish," Gregg commented.

Something fluttered in Shannon's stomach as she wondered about Gregg's interest in

Trish. With her red hair and green eyes, Trish was pretty. Maybe she had misread Gregg's reaction to her the previous summer. "I think she's fun in a strange sort of way."

"That's a good description of her. I think I'd go crazy dating someone like her, but things seem to happen when she's around."

"It sounds like you know her pretty well." She almost asked Gregg about Trish's dire predictions for Black Wednesday, but it was time for their team to be reviewed.

Shannon sat in between Lynda and Franny on the floor. Gregg stood on one side of the television with Coach Reeder on the other. While the coach critiqued the offensive strategy in the scrimmage, Lynda kept grinning at Shannon.

"I guess he doesn't hate you," she whispered.

Shannon shrugged. She wasn't sure what to think. Gregg had acted as though nothing unpleasant had happened between Monday and this afternoon. For all she knew, he could have a split personality. The good Gregg Warner liked to tease her about Hamilton High and life in Jewell Hall, while the bad Gregg Warner couldn't wait to humiliate her on the field.

She told herself she shouldn't be surprised; boys were always changing their minds. Her mistake had been thinking Gregg was more mature than the other boys she knew; but he was just like her classmate Kenny Mead, who had almost made her crazy last year acting as if he liked her one day and then ignoring her the next.

As the tape rolled, Coach Reeder patiently pointed out the scoring opportunities that had been missed, offering suggestions on how each of the offensive players could improve. Like the other coach, he backed up the tape to demonstrate the worst errors, and Shannon saw some of her teammates cringe. Being criticized in public was never fun.

"Your turn," Coach Reeder told Gregg. "The defense is your specialty."

Gregg rewound the tape and then fast-forwarded through the parts of the scrimmage that didn't apply to the defensive squad. He began with a comment for Trish, who played in the backfield with Shannon.

"DeVere, you have to watch the ball. You should have had that one."

Shannon glanced at Trish, who rolled her eyes toward the ceiling as though she'd heard it all before.

"Nelson, keep your head up when you kick. Larimer, you can't block a goal when you're standing in the corner."

"But—" Lynda started to try to defend herself, but it was useless.

Gregg kept going. "Nelson, you should have headed that ball. Good soccer players don't duck."

Shannon felt herself start to blush for what seemed like the hundredth time since she'd arrived at camp.

Gregg forged on with his criticism, not noticing how uncomfortable he was making the team—or not caring, it seemed to Shannon. "Stern, I know you're not used to playing defense, but you have to pay attention even when the ball is at the other end of the field. Do your nails on your own time."

The girls giggled while Franny studied her manicure. She wasn't going to let Gregg or anyone else see if his comment had bothered her.

"DeVere, good move there. That's keeping your eye on the ball. Nelson." He shook his head. "How are we going to get you to speed up?"

Shannon tried to hide her face by leaning forward and running her hand through her hair. It seemed as if their session was lasting forever—and every other criticism concerned her. If she was so terrible, how had their team won? Gregg made it sound as though she could single-handedly lose a game for her team. She was glad that most of the girls waiting for their turn in front of the TV were too bored to pay much attention to Mexico's playing.

Finally, he stopped the tape and ejected it from the machine. "That's it. Now, that wasn't so bad, was it?" he asked, smiling at them.

As the others groaned, Shannon jumped to her feet and headed for the door.

Gregg was at her side before she could escape. "I thought we could get a soda or something," he suggested, still holding the humiliating tape in his hand.

Shannon sucked in her breath and counted to ten. She didn't want to say anything that might get her kicked out of camp. Why was he asking her out, anyway? Could there be some comments about her playing that were so embarrassing that he had to say them in private? "No, thanks," she told him calmly.

"Aren't you thirsty?" he asked.

"No," Shannon lied. Her throat was burning from the emotions she was trying to hold back, but she would rather die from thirst than accept a soda from Benedict Arnold. "I've got to go," she said.

He stood back, giving her space to move past him. "I'm sorry."

He was sorry? She was sorry she had ever let her guard down! She should have listened to those little warnings in the back of her head; instead, she had chosen to have a few laughs with him.

Well, she knew how to handle the Gregg Warner problem. From now on, he would see hotter defensive plays by her than he had ever witnessed in his life. "Nelson" was going to play so well that he wouldn't be able to find one thing to criticize. Tomorrow—and the next day, and the next—she was going to make him admit he'd been wrong about her.

Chapter Six

"Are you going to help us or not, Shannon?"

She wasn't sure what to say. Trish's plan made sense, and if anyone except Trish had suggested it Shannon would have agreed in a minute. But so many people had warned her never to get involved in Trish's schemes.

"Did you like the way Gregg Warner trashed you yesterday?" Trish demanded.

"What do you think?" Shannon pursed her lips when she thought about how harshly Gregg had criticized her every move on the videotape.

"I think you're going to feel a lot better if you have a chance to pay him back," Trish surmised.

Shannon shook her head, still not convinced it would pay to be Trish's partner in crime.

"If you aren't the one assigned to Gregg, who should it be? Lynda?"

"Wait a minute," Lynda spoke up from the other side of their room. "I never said I was going to be part of this deal."

Trish shrugged and turned to Shannon. "I really don't see anyone else for the job, then. You have to get revenge now, or else he'll just keep humiliating you."

When Trish had explained how yesterday's rough critique session had just been part of the camp routine, Shannon had felt like a fool. The older girl knew from last year that the coaches used the films to shake up the campers and make them work harder. But all Shannon could think about was how Gregg had saved her a seat and been so friendly before he set out to embarrass her in front of a huge crowd.

"You know, it really wasn't fair for Gregg to use any of us that way," Trish added. "As if we're punching bags or something!"

No one had to tell Shannon how unfairly she had been treated by Gregg. Trish was right. Shannon wasn't going to feel better until she paid him back. "All right, I'll help you," she told Trish.

Trish grinned. "Good. I'll be back for you in a few minutes after I take care of some details."

"How could you?" Lynda asked the second Trish closed the door behind her. "Remember all the things Susie and Gregg and the others said about Trish, not to mention Darla's warning? And she should know, she's a counselor."

"Maybe she just doesn't like Trish," Shannon suggested, not willing to rethink her decision.

"And Susie and Gregg? You think they were trying to turn you against Trish, too?"

Shannon threw her hands in the air. "Who knows? I'll never understand why Gregg Warner does anything!"

Lynda got up from her chair and stood with her arms folded across her chest. "Would you just lighten up about Gregg?"

Shannon tapped her right ear. "Did you tell me to lighten up? Look, after what he did to me yesterday, he deserves what Trish has in mind for him. In fact, he probably deserves something much, much worse."

"Why?" Lynda argued. "What has he done that's so terrible besides buy you a double chocolate malt at Burger Heaven?"

"Are you kidding?" Shannon asked her roommate. The list of offenses was so long that it made her head spin. "Nelson, put your head up. Nelson, you're too slow. Nelson, don't duck. . . ."

"Coaches always say those kinds of things," Lynda reminded her. "Do you get this mad at your Hamilton High coach?"

"Coach Piper is hard to please, but he's equally nasty to everyone," Shannon explained. He even made Deb the star player, run laps when he thought she wasn't being serious about practice.

"And you think Gregg has unjustly singled you out."

Shannon could tell her roommate didn't believe that theory, but she couldn't imagine how Lynda had missed Greg's insults—there were so many of them. "You were there yesterday. You heard the things he said about me."

"Yes, I did," Lynda said slowly. "I heard him make some comments on how you could play better. And I heard him suggest how I could be a stronger goalie. And I heard him critique Trish's performance. Do I need to go on?"

"I heard all that too. But my name came up two or three times as often as anyone else's." Shannon's face grew warm just remembering how often he had yelled *Nelson*!

Lynda shook her head. "I don't think so."

"Well, Trish heard the same things I did." Shannon wasn't going to let her roommate talk her out of being angry, though she'd been trying to do exactly that ever since the tape session.

"Maybe." Lynda picked up her shin guards from the floor and started to put them on. "But I was thinking Trish would have said anything to get you to help her. She needs you!"

Shannon laughed at the ridiculous suggestion. "Half the team is in on this. What difference would it make whether or not I was part of the plan?"

"You're the one who can get the closest to Gregg," Lynda pointed out.

Shannon wanted to disagree with Lynda, but she was too confused. Sometimes Gregg did things that made it seem as if he liked her. And other times he said things that made it clear she wasn't special to him in any way. She didn't doubt she would be able to get close to Gregg after practice, but it was silly to think Trish had singled her out for that reason.

"Shan-non!" Trish called from the hall. She opened the door and dangled a bag of balloons through the crack. "It's time for us to get to work!"

*　　*　　*

"Three laps around the field," Coach Reeder ordered as practice opened. In spite of the humid ninety-degree heat, all the girls started jogging at a fairly fast pace.

"I don't get it," they heard Gregg telling the coach. "No one's complaining."

Trish looked over her shoulder and winked at Shannon. She smiled back at the redhead. As long as the cooler on the side of the field was filled with water balloons instead of juice boxes, they could all keep smiling.

When they were through running laps, Gregg wiped his forehead and said, "We need more practice with our defense. Larimer, you can sit out for a few minutes. Harper, Lucas, and Sullivan, you will be the attackers. Nelson and DeVere . . . try to keep them from scoring without the benefit of Larimer in the goal."

Shannon opened her mouth to argue when she saw the crooked grin on his face. To her, he was suggesting she and Trish wouldn't have a chance against the team's top three scorers. Behind her, Trish coughed into her hand and Shannon remembered it was vital for her to keep her temper. Biting her tongue, she flashed him a smile and said, "No problem."

Gregg looked from one girl to the next, obviously surprised by their cooperation. "I don't understand it, but it's nice to have a team full of happy campers," he joked.

They all groaned and got into their positions. Trish and Shannon fended off the forwards' shots for almost five minutes before Samantha finally scored on them. Instead of complimenting their excellent defensive work, Gregg simply said, "Take a minute or two to catch your breath and then we'll run through it all again."

Shannon sighed and pushed her damp hair off her sweaty forehead. The other girls sat down cross-legged and stared glumly at the field until Trish made a sly gesture with her shoulder toward the cooler. Then they all smiled. When Shannon thought about getting back at Gregg, not just for yesterday's video critique but for working them to death on such a hot afternoon, she felt much better.

On the sideline, Gregg clapped his hands together. "Coach Reeder says it's time to get back to work!"

Trish moved close to Shannon and nudged her in the ribs with her elbow. "Coach Reeder? Yeah, right. I bet this is all Gregg's idea."

Shannon squinted up at the slightly taller girl. If Gregg said it was the coach's idea, it must have been. Why would he lie? He might

72

not be her favorite person, but she couldn't blame him for everything that was wrong in the world.

The three girls had little problem scoring against Trish and Shannon the second time. Shannon was just too hot and tired to run. Expecting Gregg to yell at her for not working hard enough, she folded her hands and waited for the insults when he whistled for them to stop playing.

"I guess that's enough for today," he announced.

Shannon stared at Gregg. Was he really going to let them go back to the dorm and hit the showers without tearing them apart first?

"He's right," Coach Reeder agreed. "It's been a good practice. Rest up for your game tomorrow morning."

Trish bolted for the cooler and flipped open the lid. The other girls crowded around to hide the bulging water balloons from Gregg and Coach Reeder.

The coach slowly approached the huddle. "Do you have anything in there for me? I'm really thirsty."

"Sure, Coach." Trish turned quickly and threw a water balloon at his wide chest. It exploded on impact and soaked his shirt.

Shannon hid four balloons behind her back

and started after Gregg before he could see what had happened to the coach. He smiled when he saw her coming toward him.

"Hi, Shannon," he said.

"Hi, Gregg." She reached back and, gathering all of her strength, she hurled the first balloon right at him.

"What?" He tried to jump out of the way, but he wasn't quite fast enough. The balloon slapped against his bare leg. "Ooh! It's freezing cold!" he complained.

Shannon smiled. Trish had been smart to put ice in the cooler with the balloons.

"What's going on?" he asked.

"Don't you know? I thought you knew everything," she told him as she transferred another balloon to her right hand. While he tried to figure out what she was talking about, Shannon nailed him on the shoulder with her second bomb. His white Fire Lake shirt was drenched.

Out of the corner of her eye, Shannon saw Coach Reeder running across the field. A pack of girls was chasing him, and the coach was actually laughing each time a balloon hit him.

While she watched the coach, Gregg moved a few steps closer to her. "How many more balloons do you have?" he asked.

Shannon grinned at him. "Wouldn't you like to know?"

"I bet you're out of ammunition." He inched closer. "Otherwise you would have hit me again by now."

Not necessarily, Shannon thought. She could pretend she was letting him come near her so she could improve her chances to really soak him with her last two balloons, but it wouldn't be true. She just wanted to see the twinkle in his eyes up close.

"Watch out!" he cried suddenly. "There's a bee."

His right hand swished past her nose. As Shannon frantically looked around, trying to see what was happening, Gregg reached behind her with his free hand. Before she figured out his trick, he had eased a red balloon out of her grasp.

With the balloon in his possession, Gregg scrambled backward to a distance where he apparently felt safe. "You look hot, Shannon. Wouldn't you like some nice, refreshing water to cool you off?"

She stared at the red balloon he was holding over his head. How had she fallen for a stupid *bee* routine? Well, he was right about her being hot, but she would rather stretch out on her bunk with a cold can of soda than be doused with ice-cold water.

"You don't want to throw that at me," she warned him.

"Why not? You were nice enough to cool me down. I just want to return the favor," he said with a wicked grin.

Suddenly she remembered she was still holding the last balloon. If she could knock the red balloon out of his hand, he wouldn't have a weapon left to use against her. Shannon cranked her arm back and threw the balloon overhand. It arched into the air and looked like it was heading directly for its target.

At the last second, Gregg flicked the red balloon out of his hand.

As she watched her balloon harmlessly soar above his head, the red balloon exploded on her stomach before she could move out of the way. "Agh!" Shannon cried. Her shorts and shirt were soaked with the ice-cold water. She felt as though she had fallen into a snowbank.

"How could you!" she cried.

Gregg rocked back on his heels and burst out laughing. He laughed so hard and so loud that her teammates turned to stare at them. But instead of noticing how wet Gregg was, they all pointed at her and giggled.

Gregg finally caught his breath. "What do you mean, how could I? You're the one who started this whole thing!" he said, trying to peel his wet shirt away from his chest.

"Yeah, well, you deserve it for the way you've been treating me," Shannon retorted.

"When have I done anything to deserve this?" He wrung his shirt between his hands, and water dripped onto the ground.

"Only every time we're on the field! And then there's yesterday." She looked him straight in the eye.

His mouth fell open in disbelief and he walked toward her. "You're upset about a little objective criticism? I've just been trying to make you a better soccer player."

He sounded so sincere that Shannon wasn't sure what to think. While she tried to sort things out, he reached over and lifted away a strand of hair that had stuck to her wet cheek.

Shannon saw the rest of her team coming in their direction. Determined to hold onto the last shreds of her pride, she batted his hand away—but not before the others had seen him gently touch her face.

"Geez, Shannon. I wasn't trying to be a matchmaker when I asked you to take care of Gregg," Trish grumbled as she walked past them, pretending to be upset that Shannon had sold out on her friends.

Gregg covered his mouth with his hand, but Shannon could tell he was smiling. "I should have known it was Trish's idea."

"Go ahead and say it." Shannon sighed. "Tell me again how I should never get involved in any of her crazy plans."

"Maybe it was all right this time, but you owe me one now," he said.

Shannon told herself not to get excited. She tried to remember how angry he had made her the past few days, but all she could think about was the way the sun made his hair look even blonder. And his smile was so inviting. "Exactly what do I owe you?" she asked.

"How about tomorrow night?"

"Excuse me?" Shannon swallowed hard, wondering what he wanted from her.

"Some of the guys are renting movies for tomorrow night and we're going to show them in the living room in the coaches' dorm," Gregg explained.

"And you want me to . . . " She was going to ask if he wanted her to be his date, but she couldn't get the words out.

"Watch the movies with me," he concluded,

neatly avoiding the date question. "Would you like to?"

Shannon took a deep breath, trying to slow her pounding heartbeat. She had to be crazy to consider accepting his invitation. This was the guy who kept humiliating her on the field . . . and even off the field, like at the video-tape session. But they seemed to get along so well when soccer wasn't involved. As long as they weren't sports movies . . .

She took another look at his handsome face. Knowing it might be a mistake, she asked, "What time do they start?"

Chapter Seven

"It's great to hear from you, Mom." Shannon tapped her foot impatiently on the floor. It was nice to talk to someone at home, but not when Gregg was picking her up in fifteen minutes and she was only half ready.

"We've been busy," her mother continued. "April did very well in her concert last night."

"I'm glad." Shannon smiled. When her younger sister played in a concert, it was hard to even see her in the back of the percussion section. How could her mother tell whether or not April even *played* in the concert?

"And your father has been golfing nearly every afternoon. The weather has been wonderful here."

"It's been so hot here." Shannon wondered if she could put on her mascara while she talked on the phone. She decided not to risk jabbing herself in the eye.

"How hot?" Her mother sounded worried.

"In the nineties."

"Oh no! Are you drinking plenty of liquids?" Shannon knew she had said the wrong thing. If she wanted to get off the phone in the next decade, she never should have mentioned the temperature. "Mom, I'm fine."

"You always say that. Remember when you fell out of the Heppelmans' apple tree and said you were fine? Didn't you have that cast on your broken arm most of the summer?"

"Yes, Mother. But I'm not eight years old any more. Trust me," Shannon said.

"I don't know, honey. It sounds like you have something else on your mind," Mrs. Nelson observed.

"Actually, Mom, there's this guy at camp. And we—"

"You have a date!" her mother cried.

"Well, I'm not sure it's a date," Shannon hurried to explain. If she didn't set her mother straight, Mrs. Nelson would tell all the relatives at the next barbecue that Shannon had a boyfriend at soccer camp.

"Don't be shy, dear. Tell me all about him," Mrs. Nelson requested.

"He's just this guy." Across the room, Lynda raised her eyebrows at Shannon's description. "He's from Victoria. He goes to Jefferson High. We got to know each other because we're from the same town."

"What's his name?"

"Mother, his name isn't important. But he is picking me up in a few minutes, and I have naked eyes."

"Not naked eyes?" her mother teased. "Then you'd better go make yourself beautiful right away."

"Thanks, Mom."

"I'll call you once more before we pick you up next weekend. But we'd sure like to get a letter from you."

"I mailed one yesterday." Since Shannon hadn't mentioned Gregg in the letter, it had been a pretty short one. She knew her parents weren't that interested in how many headers she could do in one afternoon.

"We'll look for it then," her mother promised. "I love you, honey. Have fun on your date tonight."

Before Shannon could protest that Gregg did not consider it a date, her mother had said goodbye and hung up the phone. She stared at the receiver.

"What are you doing?" Lynda shouted from the window. "I can see Gregg on the sidewalk. You better hurry!"

Shannon's stomach began to churn when she walked into the living room in the coaches' dorm. The VCR perched on top of the television console looked suspiciously like the machine the coaches had used to show those terrible videotapes Wednesday afternoon.

"You wouldn't be showing soccer tapes, would you?" she asked Gregg.

Gregg put his hand gently over her mouth. "It's Friday night. We don't say the S word."

Shannon nodded, pretending not to notice how soft his fingertips felt against her cheek. When he removed his hand, she said, "Sounds good to me. Any other rules for tonight?"

"No water balloons."

She lifted both hands and showed him her empty palms.

"Good. Actually, the only requirement is that you be nice to me," Gregg said, smiling at her.

"Hey, Gregg! Sit down so we can get started!" Gregg's friend Steve yelled.

Gregg took Shannon's hand and guided her around the couch. He grabbed two oversized pillows and dropped them to the floor. "Have a seat, Shannon."

She rested her back against the edge of the couch and hugged a pillow in front of her, while Gregg sat on his pillow. Someone hit the "play" button and the music to *Teen Hero*, one of the previous summer's biggest movies, filled the room.

"I love that song," Gregg whispered.

"Who sings it?" Shannon whispered back.

"Jaguar. They're my absolutely favorite group."

"My sister has their poster hanging over her bed," Shannon told him. "She *loves* the drummer."

"Me, too." When Shannon raised her eyebrows comically, he added, "I mean, I have their poster, too. But I'm not attached to the drummer."

"Good."

"What band do you like?"

"It's dumb," she warned him.

"You can tell me. . . . " His arm slipped behind her, but it didn't actually touch her shoulder.

"Weird Al."

Gregg coughed to hide his laughter when she named the guy who loved to put funny words to other performers' music.

"Shhh!" someone behind them ordered.

The movie was starting and it seemed as though several of the guys and their dates wanted to see *Teen Hero*. Everyone seemed interested in the movie except Gregg. He kept leaning close to Shannon to whisper jokes about the main character. When he said the lead actor had a nose like an alligator, Shannon laughed out loud.

"Be quiet!" the person behind her whispered.

Shannon did the only thing she could think of doing, since Gregg seemed determined to crack jokes throughout the movie. She wrapped her arms around her big pillow and buried her face in it. Now if she laughed the sound would be muffled. But there was an unexpected benefit to her strategy. Just a few minutes after she leaned forward, Gregg rested his hand on her back and started making lazy circles between her shoulder blades.

Her skin tingled underneath her blouse. Any kind of back rub after a long week of practice would have been nice, but this was wonderful! She thought of turning her head to tell him she liked what he was doing, but she didn't want to move.

Half an hour later the lights came on as the credits ran across the screen. A familiar voice called, "Time for popcorn! Who wants to help me nuke it?"

A guy Shannon didn't recognize jumped to his feet to help Trish with her microwave popcorn packets. Shannon crossed her fingers and hoped that Trish wouldn't say anything that would embarrass either her or Gregg.

"Want something to drink?" Gregg asked. "There's a soda machine in the hall."

Shannon stood up and smoothed out her baggy shorts. "I'll come with you."

Although it had been nice sitting close to Gregg on the living room floor, it felt very good to stretch her legs. She looked around when they got into the hallway. "This isn't so different."

"What are you talking about?" Gregg jingled the coins in his pocket before he pulled out several quarters.

"The dorm. I thought the coaches would have a nicer place to stay, but this looks a lot like Jewell Hall."

"All the dorms are the same." He pointed to the buttons along the side of the machine, letting Shannon choose her drink. "You know,

86

during the school year college students live in these buildings."

"How have you managed in a dorm room all summer?" she asked.

He took her diet soda out of the machine and opened it for her. "Mostly I've survived because I have a huge fan in my window," he explained, handing her the can of soda. "And I brought a few things from home, like my tapes and posters and stuff." Gregg turned to face her and leaned his left hand on the wall over her head.

Shannon liked the way she felt with him looking down at her. She had seen couples like that in the hall around school, the girl smiling up at the guy who was leaning against her locker.

He took a long sip of his soda and then smiled at her. "I said, tell me about your sister and the Jaguar drummer."

"Huh?" Shannon blushed, wondering just how starry-eyed she'd gotten. "Oh, uh, April's twelve. More than anything, I think she'd probably wanted to swap notes on drumming."

"So she's a musician!" Gregg said.

"If you can call it music." Shannon shook her head as she thought about the incessant pounding that came out of her sister's bedroom every night. "Sometimes it sounds like a headache."

Gregg grinned at her. "Well, when she's famous you'll be glad you put up with her— right?"

"Movie time!" Steve called.

"What are we seeing now?" Shannon asked Gregg as they hurried back to their spots on the floor.

"I think it's *Summer Romance*," Gregg said as he sat down.

Shannon stifled a giggle. Of all the movies in the world, they had to see *Summer Romance*? Lynda would never believe her.

"Uh, why are we seeing movies tonight?" she asked. "Isn't there one tomorrow during Camper's Night Out?" She settled back against the couch and was surprised—and pleased— when Gregg motioned for her to move a little closer to him.

"Sure, if you want to call it a movie. They usually have something that's been around so long that there are flickers in the film. You know, something like *Butch Cassidy and the Sundance Kid*," Gregg said.

"I guess every copy of that film has been played a million times."

"At least!"

The film started and this time they both knew to be quiet. When a popcorn bowl was passed in their direction, they piled handfuls onto a napkin on Shannon's pillow. In order for Gregg to reach the food easily, Shannon shifted a little closer to him. It was amazing how comfortably she fit into the space under his outstretched right arm.

When the movie got romantic, some of the guys started to hoot. Cuddled next to Gregg, Shannon felt a little awkward watching the kissing scenes.

She was startled when Gregg reached out to push her hair back from her face and tuck it behind her ear. When he shifted his weight and leaned his face close to hers, Shannon was afraid to let herself think he might kiss her. She told herself her imagination was going wild because of the movie.

Then his hand curved around her neck, and he gently turned her face toward his. Gregg's lips seemed to stop a mere fraction of an inch from her own. Couldn't he decide whether or not he wanted to kiss her? Or was he waiting for her to do something? She'd been kissed a few times before, but never like this.

In the dim light from the television set, she

gazed into his eyes. He was watching her, and suddenly Shannon knew he'd been waiting for her to look up and let him know she wanted him to kiss her. She gave him a small smile and inched forward to close the space between them.

Suddenly the lights were switched on. "Body check!" Trish yelled. "I want to know who's getting romantic ideas from this movie."

Gregg pulled away from Shannon, but not before they had been spotted.

"Hey, Warner!" Steve called out.

Another counselor asked, "Who's your friend?"

"It's Shannon Nelson," Trish answered. "I don't believe my eyes!" she quipped.

"A *camper*?" one guy asked, sounding shocked. "Warner, the female counselors have been complaining that you've been ignoring them. Do I have to tell them that they lost out to a camper?"

"And one from his own team!" Steve observed. Gregg rolled his eyes, flushing, and Shannon knew he was going to have a few choice words for his good friend Steve later.

"Isn't *that* convenient?" the other guy asked.

"Excuse me, but I want to see the rest of

the movie," someone's girlfriend said, to Shannon's great relief.

"Okay, Trish, get rid of the lights," Steve requested. "We've had our thrill for tonight."

Gregg arranged his pillow against the couch and leaned back on it. He looked angry and Shannon knew the magic between them was gone. She tucked her pillow behind her back. Shannon turned her eyes to the screen, but she didn't see another second of the movie. All she could think about were the hundred different ways she would tell Trish off for spoiling such a perfect moment.

Chapter Eight

"Aren't you getting ready for Camper's Night Out?" Shannon asked her roommate the next evening. She had been trying to get her hair just right for almost half an hour. Why was Lynda lounging on her bed?

"I'm not going," Lynda answered.

"Why not?"

"My mom is supposed to call tonight and I don't want to miss her." Lynda's cheeks turned pink.

"Is something special going on?" Lynda hadn't said a whole lot about her family, and all Shannon really knew was that she had a pesty little brother.

"Nothing special," she said quietly. "I'm just a little homesick."

Shannon sat on the edge of Lynda's bed.

"Hey, I didn't know. Are you going to be all right?"

"I'll be a lot better after I talk to my mom," Lynda said with a hopeful smile.

"But what are you going to do after she calls? I hate to leave you here all alone. Maybe I should stay. I'm not going to miss much at the gym."

"Oh, really? What about Gregg?"

"I doubt he'll be waiting for me," Shannon said, thinking of the disaster the night before. She was sort of hoping Gregg would be at the party in the gym, but he hadn't been very friendly at practice that afternoon. In fact, he hadn't even criticized her once. It wasn't normal.

"If you're not thinking about Gregg, why did you just spend half an hour on your hair?" Lynda asked. She reached out to touch Shannon's hair and grinned. "You know, it feels a little like cotton candy."

Shannon giggled. "That's what happens with five layers of hairspray. I was trying to get the crimped look," she explained. "Guess I got carried away."

"Want me to help you?" Lynda offered with a smile.

Shannon flicked her hair over her shoulder. "Is there hope for me?"

"You need to get out the hairspray with a little shampoo while I get my gel ready." Lynda hurried over to her dresser and started sorting through the bottles on top of it.

Shannon sat on the bed and looked at Lynda. Why was she thinking of herself when her roommate was the one who was so sad? "I'll only let you do this if you promise to come over to the gym after you talk to your mom. I don't want you to sit around here all night getting lonely. Going to a party might cheer you up."

"I'll see," Lynda said. *"Maybe* I'll come over, but no promise."

"Knock, knock," a much-too-familiar voice called from the hall. Their door opened, and Trish came inside with her hands covering her face. "Am I safe here?"

Shannon had pointedly ignored Trish all day. The girl had a lot of nerve coming to her room. Shannon knew that if she still had a hairbrush in her hand, there would have been fifty-fifty odds on her aiming it at Trish's head. Instead she said, "How could you?"

"Hey, I was just fooling around. I didn't know I was going to catch you and Gregg getting all cozy."

Shannon bit her lip to keep from saying things she would later regret. No one like

Gregg Warner had ever kissed her before, and Trish had ruined it. Still, she didn't hate Trish. "I'm not sure he'll ever talk to me again," she told her, hoping the other girl would understand how terrible she felt.

"Don't be silly. Really embarrassing situations can bring people together." When Shannon gave Trish a look of disbelief, she said, "It's like the two of you share something, a painful experience, that hasn't happened to anyone else."

"Painful is the right word for it!" Shannon exclaimed.

"No, but she's right," Lynda volunteered with sudden enthusiasm. "In sixth grade my best friend Martha and I were caught peeking at the answers to a math test . . . well, we didn't mean to peek, we were actually just looking for a red pen—"

"But no one believed you," Trish interrupted. "I've been there before!"

"Right—especially not Mrs. Curtis, my teacher," Lynda continued.

Shannon winced when she thought about how awful Lynda and her friend must have felt. "I bet you never wanted to set foot in school again."

"That's for sure." Lynda smiled. "But

Martha and I have been good friends ever since that day!"

"And you think that can happen for Gregg and me?" Shannon desperately wanted to believe Lynda and Trish were right.

"It's worth a try," Trish said. "But if I were you, I'd do something about my hair. It looks like you have a whole can of spray on it."

Shannon glanced at Lynda and giggled. "You could say that."

Trish smiled. "Am I forgiven?"

It was tempting to say that would depend on how Gregg acted at the party, but Shannon couldn't be that selfish. After all, Trish hadn't meant to ruin her chances. "Yeah. We're still friends."

Trish breathed a sigh of relief. "Thanks. I was really feeling bad about what happened. Hey, I've got to get ready for the party. If I see Gregg hanging around, I'll send him in your direction."

Considering Trish's record with Gregg, Shannon wasn't sure she needed any help from her. "If you don't mind, Trish, maybe you should stay out of his way tonight."

Trish winked. "No problem. See you there!"

Shannon laughed when she saw the poster on the front door of the gym: *Movie starts promptly at 7:00 in room 229—Butch Cassidy and the Sundance Kid.*

"What's so funny?" Franny inquired.

"The movie!"

Franny sighed. "It's one of my favorites. I *love* Robert Redford."

"So does my mom," Shannon said quietly. It seemed ironic that the first thing she saw in the gym that night made her automatically think of Gregg.

Franny giggled self-consciously. "I know I should be drooling over someone younger like Tom Cruise, but my mom started taking me to Robert Redford films when I was six years old."

"I think he's great," Shannon said quickly. She hadn't meant to make Franny feel silly for liking Redford. "It's just that I've seen it so many times."

"If you don't mind, I think I'll stay for the movie," Franny said, edging toward the stairs. "Maybe I'll see you later."

"Enjoy the show!" Shannon called as she headed down the hall to explore the other activities.

The basketball court was open, but it was crowded with tall boys all fighting over the ball. Shannon didn't mind tossing a ball at a hoop once in a while, but the boys racing down the court looked too competitive for her. Cindy, her friend back in Victoria, would probably say the odds were fantastic: approximately a dozen boys to one girl. But Shannon knew she would probably just make a fool of herself.

She continued walking in the direction of loud voices coming from further down the hall. She followed the sound and discovered herself on a balcony overlooking a pool. She hadn't realized there would be swimming.

"Hey, Shannon!" someone called from the water below.

She squinted at the pool until she found the person waving to her. It was Susie, the girl she had met at Burger Heaven the first day. "Hi!" Shannon answered.

"Come on down. The water feels great!" Susie yelled.

Shannon pointed to her mint-green shirt and white shorts. "I didn't bring my suit."

"Go back and get it," Susie invited her.

"Maybe I will." But Shannon decided to see what else was happening first. She hadn't seen Gregg, and swimming was out of the question until she found him. Lynda had done a great job of fixing up her hair with just the right amount of gel. She would never be able to reconstruct the look on her own.

Shannon hadn't seen too many fellow campers yet. There had to be something else going on in the building, unless *Butch Cassidy and the Sundance Kid* had drawn a record crowd. As she strolled down the hall, she finally heard the unmistakable beat of rock music. It led her to the open area outside the locker rooms.

Someone had cranked a boombox up to full volume, and couples were dancing all over the hall. Others were standing against the walls, talking and moving to the beat. Shannon recognized several faces, but she didn't see anyone she knew well enough to actually approach.

Then she saw Gregg at the end of one row of lockers. Determined to be optimistic, she walked up to him with a big smile on her face. "Hi, Gregg! How's it going?"

He turned away from his buddies and faced her. His blue eyes usually sparkled when he saw her—at least in social situations—but not tonight. "How are you tonight, Shannon?" he said with very little enthusiasm.

"I'm—okay." She didn't want to let him discourage her, but it was hard to overlook his less-than-friendly mood. Shannon took two steps closer, operating on Trish's theory that their humiliating experience could bring them closer to each other. "Still bummed out about what happened last night?" she bluntly asked him.

He looked surprised that she had chosen to bring up the matter. "I lost a little sleep over it, but I'll be fine."

She thought he sounded a little strange, and she couldn't help remembering how he had leaned over her at the soda machine the night before. It was probably crazy, but she wished he would do the same thing right now. The only better idea he might have would be dancing. She bet it would be great to dance with him.

"I liked the movies. Thanks for inviting me." She hadn't had a chance to thank him last night. He had rushed off without even saying good-night.

He cleared his throat. "You're welcome."

A new song started on the radio and Shannon recognized it as Jaguar's newest hit. Gathering every last ounce of her courage she reached out for his hand. "This song is super. Let's dance."

When she took a step toward the dancers, Gregg didn't come with her. In fact, his feet seemed to be rooted to the floor. Shannon had the sinking feeling that she had made a major mistake, but she tried to ignore her pounding heart. "Gregg? Are you coming or not? Isn't this your favorite group?"

"Actually, I have to work tonight. See that girl over there?" He pointed to a definite wallflower. "It's my job to cheer her up."

His job? If he was supposed to be keeping the campers happy, he was failing miserably in her case. She gritted her teeth and watched him cross the hall and speak to the girl. It was no surprise to Shannon when the girl smiled at him. Gregg Warner could be very charming—when he wanted to be.

She slumped against the wall. Gregg was acting as if he wanted to forget Friday night had ever happened.

She saw Brent and waved to him. He smiled. Seeing a friendly face made Shannon feel a little better.

"Hi, Shannon," Brent said as he approached her. "How is half of Mexico's best defense?"

"What's that supposed to mean?" Shannon asked crossly.

He blinked in surprise. "I think it was a compliment."

Shannon shook her head. "I'm sorry, Brent. Guess I'm feeling a little defensive these days."

Chuckling, Brent told her, "That's good. The defensive star is on the defensive." Shannon laughed in spite of herself. Then

Brent cleared his throat. "Uh, is the other half around tonight? I mean, is Lynda coming?"

"No. Well, maybe later. Her mom was supposed to call," Shannon explained. "I guess I feel kind of lonely without her to hang out with."

"You do seem kind of down," Brent observed. "But I have the perfect remedy. Would you like to dance?"

She glanced at Gregg and the so-called wallflower one more time. They were both laughing about something. In fact, the poor girl seemed to be having a *great* time with Gregg. Well, Shannon thought she certainly had better things to do than wait for Gregg to cheer *her* up. "Sure, Brent," she said.

The next song on the radio station was one with a Latin beat. It was easy to dance to, and Brent was a good dancer. For the first few minutes, Shannon hoped Gregg would notice how good she looked. She had been told that her long wavy hair moved in a pretty way when she danced. She wanted Gregg to see her and to regret that she was dancing with Brent instead of him.

As she and Brent moved down the hall with the rest of the dancers, she lost sight of Gregg. She concentrated on her dancing. It felt great to let go of her worries and let the music take over.

"You're a really good dancer," Brent told her after three long, fast songs. "Are you thirsty?"

Shannon put her hand to her incredibly dry throat and nodded.

He pointed back to the area where they had started dancing. "I think there's a snack bar down there. Let it be my treat."

"Thanks."

Shannon saw Gregg up ahead in the crowd. As they passed him, she watched Brent's face closely and pretended to be hanging on his every word.

But she didn't have to pretend to be interested when Brent asked, "How would you like to go to the High-Flying Waterslide with me tomorrow?"

"A-a waterslide?" Shannon stammered. Although she had enjoyed dancing with Brent, she wasn't interested in being anything more than friends with him. Her heart was so tangled up with Gregg Warner that she couldn't begin to get interested in someone else so soon. Still, he was a very nice guy, and she didn't want to hurt his feelings. "I don't know," she muttered.

"Don't you swim?"

"Sure! Like a fish," she told him. The swim coach at Hamilton High had tried to talk her into joining the swim team, but she couldn't imagine spending that much time in the water. She didn't want to wrinkle up like a prune at the age of sixteen.

"Then why don't you want to go?" Brent asked.

"Well . . ." Shannon hesitated, wondering how to make her point politely. "It was fun dancing with you, but—"

"Shannon, I know what you're thinking. But I'm not asking you on a date," he explained with a crooked smile. "A lot of kids from camp are going. I thought you might like to come along with us. In fact, bring a friend."

"Like Lynda?" Shannon guessed with a sly grin.

His eyes lit up, and Shannon could tell that he liked her roommate. Lynda should have come to the party, but she had gotten a date anyway, without even being there! "We'll be there tomorrow," Shannon promised. "Where and what time?"

He told her they would meet in front of the dining hall after the morning practice. It still surprised Shannon that the slave-driving coaches actually gave the campers Sunday afternoon off for a little rest and relaxation. Brent made her promise again to invite Lynda, and Shannon couldn't agree with him fast enough.

He wanted to dance some more, but Shannon was anxious to get back to her roommate. She hated to think of Lynda moping around the room and she wanted to share the good news immediately.

"I'll see you tomorrow," she said as she waved to him. "Thanks!"

He waved back at her. "We'll have a great time. Good night!"

It was a short distance back to Jewell Hall, and Shannon broke into a jog. She was too excited about her news for Lynda to walk. In her hurry, she even turned down an invitation to a pizza pig-out on the second floor of their dorm. She took the last flight of stairs two steps at a time, hoping Lynda would be in the room. To her relief, her roommate was home—and off the phone.

"We've got a date with Brent Parks tomorrow!" Shannon announced in the doorway.

"We do? What are you talking about?" Lynda looked at Shannon as if she had lost her mind. "Don't you mean *you*?"

Shannon shook her head and shut the door behind her. "Actually, he wants to be with you. I hope you don't mind that I accepted for you . . . or that I plan to tag along to High-Flying Waterslide tomorrow afternoon."

"You're kidding!" Lynda's blue eyes lit up. "You're not making this up just so I'll feel better? I mean, you don't have to do that for me. I'm fine."

"If you were fine before I came in here, you must be excellent now! Brent *is* one good-looking guy, not to mention a terrific dancer."

"How would you know?" Lynda asked, confused.

"He had to settle for me when he found out you weren't at the gym. I think he felt sorry for me after Gregg abandoned me."

"Gregg didn't pay any attention to you?"

"Only long enough to let me know he's pretty upset about last night. But I don't want to talk about him. What are you going to wear to the waterslide?"

"A swimsuit." The sparkle in Lynda's eyes told Shannon her roommate was very happy to know that Brent liked her.

"I know that! But what about a cover-up? What will you do with your hair?"

"Unlike you, I'm drip-dry." Lynda ran her fingers through her loose curls.

Shannon began to mentally ransack her closet. Even if she wasn't interested in impressing Brent, there would be other guys at the waterslide. Shannon wanted to look her best.

"If we're leaving right after morning practice, we'll have to pack gym bags and change there. Let's figure out what we'll need."

"Good idea! This should only take half the night," Shannon joked. "But it'll be worth it. I can't wait to get off this stupid campus and not think about soccer for an entire afternoon!"

Chapter Nine

"It's great here!" Lynda said as she scanned the park.

"Did you pack any sunscreen?" Shannon asked, digging through her bag.

Her heart had started hammering the minute she saw Gregg climb out of the second carload of campers, and she kept her head down as he passed by her.

"Ready to hit the slide, ladies?" Brent asked. He looked super in his jams. Shannon didn't mind that his eyes were always on Lynda. She was just glad to be included. She didn't want Gregg to see her sitting alone like some kind of loser.

"I always enjoyed coming here when I was a camper," she heard Gregg announcing as he headed for an empty beach chair.

"Gee, Gregg. I hope you can still have fun now that you're *management,*" Susie drawled loud enough for everyone to hear.

Shannon smiled. She wanted to shake Susie's hand. Gregg wasn't being himself, and she certainly wasn't impressed with the stuck-up way he was acting.

She followed Brent and Lynda up what seemed like more than a hundred steps. But it was worth it when they looked down on the slick, twisting slide. They watched as people screamed all the way down the slide and then flew into the clear blue pool at the bottom.

"Are you ready for this?" she asked Lynda.

"I'll go first," Brent told them. "I'll catch you at the bottom."

Shannon doubted he could. It didn't look easy to catch anyone, the way people were racing down the wet slide. Still, she thought it was really cute that Brent wanted to be there for Lynda.

Brent jumped onto the slide and was whisked away in seconds. Lynda looked over her shoulder at Shannon and cried, "Here I go!" Shannon gave her the thumbs-up sign.

Shannon had no one to talk to before she pushed off. There was a man with two children behind her, and she doubted they'd be interested in the butterflies in her stomach. For no one, she screamed, "Geronimo!"

She spotted Brent in the pool as she sped toward the end of the slide. He actually did try to catch Lynda. He stumbled a bit, but he managed to keep her from ducking under the water. "Watch out!" Shannon yelled, trying to warn them that she would be arriving in a few seconds.

Lynda just kept gazing into Brent's eyes until Shannon crashed into both of them. All three of them splashed into the pool, spraying water onto the deck. Shannon came up for air just in time to see Gregg giving her a look that seemed to say *how juvenile.*

Susie must have read his expression the same way. She gave him a shove and said, "Loosen up, Mr. Assistant Coach. This isn't the practice field."

"Does it bother you that she's spending so much time with him?" Lynda whispered as they climbed out of the pool.

"Not at all. Would you want to be with him today? He's really being a jerk," Shannon said. She smoothed out her towel and sat down on it.

"How perceptive of you to notice." Lynda shook her head and water sprayed in every direction. "At least you're not so lovesick that you're blind."

"Want to do it again?" Brent asked, dripping on Lynda's towel as he stood over them.

"Not right away," Lynda told him. "Pull up your towel and sit down for a while."

Not worrying about what Brent might think, Shannon slicked her hair back and slipped a headband over her forehead. She knew her hair was glued to her head, but the hot pink headband would give her a little style. She adjusted the legs on her pink, black, and white one-piece suit, then reached for the bottle of suntan lotion.

Shannon was rubbing sunscreen on her legs when a shadow fell over all three towels. She squinted up and saw Gregg. Her hopes rose for a second—then she reminded herself that he wasn't the same nice guy she had fallen for the week before.

"Nice work, Brent," he commented. "You actually have *two* dates."

"Well, I'd think a *coach* could have all the dates he wanted," Brent countered as Susie approached.

Gregg stared at Shannon and mumbled something she didn't understand.

"No, it is tougher being a coach," Susie explained, her voice full of sarcasm. "You guys have no idea how hard it is to maintain the proper image."

Shannon felt as if she had been struck by lightning. *An image!* Why hadn't she figured that out before?

She watched Gregg as he walked over to the slide with Susie. Gregg Warner thought he was pretty important being an assistant coach this year when most kids his age were still campers. Too important to be seen with a first-time camper, that was for sure! She had been fooled by his friendliness in group situations—eating at Burger Heaven, and kidding around with his friend Steve before the videotape review session. But when had he let things go past the point of mere friendship? Only when they were alone in the hall at the soda machine, and later when he had tried to kiss her in the dark. When the lights came on, there had been more than just physical distance between them. Both last night and today, he had been doing his best to make it look as though there was nothing special between him and Shannon.

Susie had explained it perfectly: Gregg was keeping up his image. Well, she hoped his *image* would keep him company when he realized he had made a mistake with her. Even if he was still interested in being with her when they were alone, Shannon didn't want a boyfriend who was embarrassed to be seen with her in public!

"Anyone want to slide again?" Brent asked.

"I'm just enjoying the sun," Lynda said.

Shannon adjusted her sunglasses. "I'd like to do it again in a little while."

"Do you mind if I hang out with the guys then?" Brent asked. "Come find me when you feel like taking the plunge."

Shannon didn't bother to answer since she knew he was waiting for Lynda's response. Her roommate told him to have a good time, and then she stretched out on her stomach.

"I've just realized the most amazing thing about Gregg," Shannon whispered when Brent was gone.

"Hmm? The sun is making me sleepy," Lynda mumbled.

"I'll tell you later." Shannon tucked her gym bag under her head and closed her eyes. After running around the soccer field all week, it felt great to relax.

"Sleeping Beauty, I presume?"

Shannon's eyes flew open behind her sunglasses. Gregg was squatting next to her, while Lynda was napping on the other side of her. Playing along with his routine, she said, "Well, if it isn't Prince Charming."

"I thought you would stick around last night until I had time to dance with you," Gregg said.

"I had other things to do." Although she

could sympathize with Gregg's position among the guys, she didn't have to put up with his attitude.

"I've seen you around with Brent, but aren't you kind of a third wheel?"

"At least I'm with people who aren't ashamed to be seen with me," she told him bluntly.

His blue eyes opened a little wider, and Shannon was glad her dark glasses were hiding her eyes. Gregg's inconsiderate comments were hurting her. It was better that he couldn't see her pain.

"You think I'm ashamed of you?"

"Oh, no. Only when anyone from camp is around," she answered.

"Maybe I just prefer being alone with you. In fact, I was thinking . . . how about meeting me by the pine tree in front of my dorm a little after midnight?" he asked.

Shannon struggled to control her temper. "I don't think so, Gregg. I have to be at practice early tomorrow morning."

"Okay . . . but I'll be there waiting for you, in case you change your mind," Gregg promised.

Turning her head, Shannon hoped he would leave. Meet him at midnight? How could he insult her that way? He was so embarrassed to be seen with her that he only wanted to be with her in the dead of night! Sure, she wanted to spend time with him, but she refused to sink so low. He was acting as if she were something he had to hide!

"Oh, boy," Lynda muttered from her towel as soon as Gregg had gone.

"You're awake?" Shannon threw her arm over her face. "Did you hear everything?"

"I sure did," Lynda said. "I'm afraid that Gregg Warner knows you like him . . . a lot."

"What could be worse?" Shannon moaned.

Wasn't it bad enough he wanted to keep her a secret? Did he need to know how much she wished things could be different?

Last winter, someone had told Kenny Mead, a boy in her class, that she had a thing about him. The boy had teased her until she tried to convince her mother that she was verging on mono and needed to stay home from school for the next month. Of course, her mother had seen through the fake and Kenny Mead eventually got tired of making kissing noises at her in English class. But she had still vowed to never again let a boy know she liked him until he put his feelings on the line first.

"I think you have to forget him. If you don't, he'll make you crazy," Lynda advised.

"You're right." As hard as it was going to be, Shannon knew what she had to do. "Starting now, Gregg Warner is just an assistant coach."

"Can you do that?"

Shannon couldn't pretend it would be easy, but she knew it was the only way she'd survive the second week of camp. "Watch me. When I'm not practicing, I'll be hanging out with the girls in the dorm. Except for you . . . you'll probably be busy with Brent."

"Someone mention my name?"

"Yes, uh, I did." Shannon sat up and slid her sunglasses off her face. Hoping Brent hadn't heard any more of their conversation, she changed the subject. "I'm ready to tackle that waterslide. I dare you to try to catch both Lynda and me this time."

"No problem," he boasted. "Willing to give it a try?" Brent asked Lynda. When she nodded, he offered her a hand and pulled her to her feet.

As they headed for the steps, Lynda laid her hand on Shannon's shoulder. "Don't worry. I know you're going to be fine."

"It doesn't hurt having a friend like you," Shannon whispered. The next few days were going to be hard, but she would survive.

Chapter Ten

"We have something different in mind this morning," Coach Reeder announced when the Mexico team assembled on the practice field first thing Monday morning.

"What? No laps?" Trish actually managed to sound disappointed. All the girls laughed. There was no chance the coach would ever forget about laps.

"We're going to start this week with a little contest."

The girls all looked to Trish. Since she seemed to know everything about the camp from previous experience, Shannon assumed the older girl would know about the contest. When Trish shrugged her shoulders, the girls looked around to see what the other teams were doing. Most were running laps.

"I don't think anyone else is having a team contest today," the coach told them. "Gregg and I cooked up this little idea to see where our strengths and weaknesses lie."

At the mention of his name, Shannon almost let her gaze stray in Gregg's direction. She shook her head to chase all thoughts of him out of her brain.

"Something wrong, Nelson?" Coach Reeder asked.

"Just a chill," she said, realizing too late how dumb her excuse must sound on a morning when it was already over eighty degrees.

"Are you sick?" Trish whispered.

"No," Shannon softly replied. "Terminally stupid."

"All right then, I'll let our assistant coach explain the contest," the coach said.

Gregg stood next to Coach Reeder and produced a clipboard from behind his back. "What we have in mind is basically a one-on-one test. Each of you will take a turn defending the goal while each of your teammates has one chance to score on you. I'll keep track of how many goals are scored on each of you, while Coach Reeder records how many times each of you manages to score."

Shannon moaned along with the rest of the girls. Gregg's contest sounded about as fair

118

as a pop quiz in history. She was a defensive player and had been since junior high. Did he expect her to get a ball into the goal when she had spent the last three years concentrating on keeping balls *out* of the net?

Samantha raised her hand. "Assistant Coach Warner? I have no idea how to play goalie."

Shannon was glad someone else was pointing out how stupid the competition sounded. She wouldn't have dared challenge Gregg.

He avoided answering the real question by explaining, "You don't have to actually stand in the goal. It's up to you to defend the goal whatever way you think will work best."

"An automatic weapon might not be bad," Trish muttered. Shannon heard her and tried to stifle her giggles. She ended up coughing.

"Nelson," the coach called, "are you *sure* you're all right?"

"I'm fine." She found it mildly amusing that Gregg wasn't concerned about her health. To protect his noninterested image, he would probably let her drop dead from heatstroke.

"If there are no more questions, let's begin," Gregg instructed.

Shannon took her place in line behind Trish to try to score on Lynda.

"This is a rotten idea," Trish complained.

"I'm going to bomb," Shannon told her.

119

"Don't give him the satisfaction!"

Shannon liked Trish's idea. Gregg was probably expecting her kicks to miss the goal by miles. Well, she was going to show him she wasn't the sloppy soccer player that he seemed to think she was. When it was her turn, she squinted at Lynda and then clenched her teeth with determination. She dribbled the ball toward the goal and then tried to slam it past her roommate. Lynda fell on the ball and easily blocked her shot.

One miss wasn't the end of the world, Shannon told herself. Besides, Lynda was a very good goalie. She would do better next time when someone with less experience was guarding the goal.

Shannon tried to kick the ball at an angle when Samantha was playing defense. She had seen the forwards score dozens of times with that technique. Unfortunately she miscalculated, and the ball flew past the goal and rolled halfway across the next practice field. The next time Shannon tried kicking the ball over the defender's head . . . and then between the defender's legs. No matter *what* she tried, the result was always the same: no goal. The only good thing about the contest was that Gregg was recording the *defender's* success; Coach Reeder was keeping the scoring statistics, and he had no reason to be prejudiced against her.

When it was finally her chance to defend the goal, Shannon felt much more comfortable. Trish was the first to dribble the ball in her direction. Since Trish was a fellow defensive player, Shannon figured she would be able to guess her moves—Trish wasn't used to playing offense, either. She was stunned when Trish shot the ball from ten yards out and it flew past her into the goal.

"I'm sorry," Trish said softly as she walked near Shannon.

"Don't worry about me," she answered. "We're all in this together."

"You're not kidding. I think this coaching stuff has gone to Gregg's head. He sure was a lot more fun last year."

"Next!" Gregg called when the short conversation delayed the competition.

"Sorry, Coach!" Trish called out in a singsong voice.

Shannon's luck didn't improve, although she tried harder and harder to stop the balls. One flew over her head, just grazing her fingertips. She couldn't help tensing when Gregg frowned and scribbled some kind of note on his clipboard. Then Shannon thought she actually had caught one ball, until it slipped out of her hands and rolled into the goal.

With clenched fists, she vowed to stop the last ball. It was a matter of pride. She ran forward to meet the ball and kick it miles away from the goal. It was a good idea until her right foot slipped out from under her. She landed on the ground with her legs stretched into a split, and the ball zipped into the net.

"I might as well pack and go home," she told Lynda when the contest was over. She hadn't scored a single point, and everyone else had managed to score on her. "I'm the worst on offense *and* defense."

"It's just a dumb contest. It doesn't matter," Lynda reassured her.

Shannon heard footsteps behind her and closed her eyes when she realized it was Gregg. "You had a rough time today," he said.

Shannon turned to face him. "You ought to know," she said harshly. There wasn't a single bone in her body that felt friendly toward Gregg Warner. She could just imagine him presenting the contest idea to Coach Reeder, knowing she would fail miserably. In fact, she wouldn't be surprised if he had come up with the idea as one more way to humiliate her in public, since that seemed to be his newest hobby.

"I was wondering if you're tired because

you waited for me by the pine tree last night," he continued.

Shannon's mouth fell open. Didn't his ego ever take a break? "Of course I wasn't there, but you should know that. You said you'd be waiting in case I changed my mind."

Gregg smiled. "I was there. I really hoped you'd come. I thought maybe you stopped by after I went back into the dorm."

"Warner!" Coach Reeder called. "Do you have your scores tallied so we can hand out the awards?"

"Awards!" Shannon moaned.

"Of course. This is a first-class contest," Gregg told her before he trotted over to the coach.

"What do you think about him now?" Lynda inquired.

"I think I hate his idea of a first-class contest."

"I'm not talking about the competition. It sounded like he really wanted to see you last night. Maybe he wasn't saying it just to tease you yesterday," Lynda suggested.

Shannon rolled her eyes. "Be serious. You were right the first time. He knows how I feel . . . I mean, how I *felt* about him. And now because I'm a 'little camper' and he's an assistant coach, he's trying to make me look like a fool."

The girls stood in a group as Gregg announced the contest winners. The third-place prize, a gift certificate for Mama's Kitchen, went to Lynda. Samantha won a new soccer ball for taking second place. And Trish received a fifty-dollar certificate for Feet, an athletic shoe store in town, for doing the best in the contest.

Shannon applauded along with the rest of the team. Although she had done horribly, she was happy for her friends.

"Just a minute," Gregg called when the girls started to leave for the dining hall. "There *is* one last prize."

Questions buzzed among the girls. He had already given the award for first place. What could be left?

"Some people might call this a booby prize," he told them. "But I'd prefer to offer it as a recognition that one member of the team sacrificed her own scores to make the rest of you look good. Shannon Nelson, this is for you."

Shannon's cheeks burned. She didn't want to take the brown lunch bag from him, but the other girls had started to giggle. And the laughter grew louder as she hesitated. Finally, she grabbed it from him. When she opened the bag, a terrible smell escaped.

"What is this?" she asked, wrinkling her nose.

"Take it out and see," Gregg told her, chuckling along with her teammates.

Shannon hesitated, then closed her eyes and stuck her hand into the bag. She felt some kind of cloth inside. She pulled it out slowly and gasped when it turned out to be someone's disgusting gym socks.

"*Gross!*" She threw the bag and the socks on the ground and pushed her way past her team members. Gregg had done it again. How convenient for him that Coach Reeder had let him help make up the contest. He had found one more way to prove to all his friends that he didn't like her. What better way than to design a contest where she was guaranteed to fail? Couldn't he prove his point without humiliating her again and again?

"Shannon, wait!" Gregg called after her.

"Just leave me alone, Gregg!" Shannon yelled, close to tears. Gregg ran after her and grabbed her shoulder. Gently he turned her toward him. "Are you mad about the prize? It was just a joke," he insisted.

"I guess I forgot to laugh." Shannon crossed her arms over her chest and stared at him.

"Hey, you *are* mad."

Give the guy a prize for intelligence, she

told herself. "How would *you* feel if someone you used to think was a friend gave you something so disgusting?" she demanded.

He squinted at her as if she were talking nonsense. "It wasn't a personal attack, Shannon. I would have given the stinky socks to anyone who came in dead last in the contest."

She groaned at his description of her performance. "I don't believe you," she said.

"What do you think?" he asked. "Do you think I knew Shannon Nelson would get shut out? Or do you think I had a different prize in mind . . . but when you turned out to be the winner I stuck these socks in a bag?" When Shannon refused to answer him, he repeated, "What do you think?"

"Who cares? All that matters is that I know what you really think about me, so you don't have to waste any more time trying to make me feel better." Shannon removed his hand from her shoulder and hurried away.

Lynda was waiting for her by the pine trees. "Are you all right?" she asked.

"He tried to tell me the award wasn't meant to be personal," she informed her roommate. "Can you believe that?"

Lynda gave the idea a moment's consideration and nodded. "That could be true."

"Come on, Lynda. Can you imagine him giving a bag of dirty socks to Trish if she'd been the one who bombed today?" Shannon argued.

The idea of offending Trish made Lynda laugh. "She would have spent the whole week finding ways to pay him back. He wouldn't have dared give her that prize."

Shannon had to laugh, too. She had picked the wrong person for her example. "Can I see your prize?"

Lynda handed over the envelope. "It's a ten-dollar gift certificate for Mama's Kitchen."

"That's the place with the great malts—well, according to Susie, anyway. But I think you have to get there by car. Does Brent have one?"

"If he does, I'll ask him to give us a ride." Lynda tapped the envelope against her palm. "I can't think of anything better than sharing my prize with you. Maybe Gregg Warner thinks you deserve used gym socks, but I think you're worth a malt."

Shannon threw her arm around Lynda's shoulder and gave her a hug. "Thanks. You're great. But I think you should use the certificate to treat Brent."

Lynda sighed. "That *does* sound fun. You won't mind if I leave you alone?"

"I'll be fine. If I can't find anything else to do, I might see what ideas Trish has for making Gregg Warner suffer."

"You're not serious." Lynda's brow wrinkled with concern.

"No." Shannon paused and reviewed her options. Revenge would be sweet, but Shannon was smart enough to realize it wouldn't make Gregg like her. Besides, she certainly didn't want him to think she was desperate! As boring as it sounded, she knew the best thing would be for her to concentrate on the soccer at camp—not the social life. After all, she had come to camp to fine-tune her soccer techniques, not to find a boyfriend.

School would start in a few weeks. There were tons of boys she hadn't met yet at Hamilton High . . . and she would bet that every last one of them would be nicer to her than Gregg Warner had been!

Chapter Eleven

"This game could be big," Franny told the other girls from Jewell Hall as they walked toward their field after lunch on Thursday.

"She's right," Trish seconded. "If we win this game and the one tomorrow, Saturday we'll be playing for the camp championship!"

"Are you kidding?" Lynda squealed.

"That's surprising, considering you've got a klutz like me on the team," Shannon said, only half-kidding.

"Are you still worrying about that stupid contest?" Trish queried. "That was three days ago. Besides, you're the best defensive player on our team."

Shannon shook her head. "Thanks for being nice, but . . ."

She sighed. The situation with Gregg was tense, with them being coldly polite to each other at practices and games. Shannon felt like her ego had taken such a beating that she wasn't sure what she could do anymore.

Trish shook her by the shoulders. "I'm not *that* nice," she informed her. "You really are good."

"That's for sure," Franny declared. When Trish gave her a look, she hurried to add, "I didn't mean you're not nice. I was talking about Shannon. I've seen her stop so many strong drives toward the goal."

"She's right," Lynda added. "You make my job so easy. The ball barely ever gets back into my territory."

"Stop it!" Shannon covered her ears with her hands. "I'm going to get a swelled head with all these compliments."

"We don't want that," Trish said, laughing. "Just make sure we win today so we can play for the championship this weekend."

It sounded like a good goal to Shannon. After giving up all hope for a summer romance, she could get into being part of the championship team. At least that way she would have something good to talk about when she got home. "I'll give it my best shot," she promised her teammates.

By the time they got to the field, the whole team was ready, and Coach Reeder's last-minute instructions just made them more psyched. Once she was in her position, Shannon couldn't stand still until the ref blew his whistle to start the game.

The Mexico team jumped on the first ball, sending all the action to the other end of the field. But the Brazil team wasn't going to give up easily; they blocked shot after shot. Shannon and Trish moved closer to the center line to be ready in case someone kicked the ball loose from the crowd. Suddenly, one of the Brazil players made a long pass to a teammate near the center line. In half a second, the girl was past both Shannon and Trish as she hurried the ball toward Lynda in the goal.

"Nelson, get on it!" Gregg yelled from the sideline, but he didn't need to tell Shannon it was her job to stop the breakaway.

She ran as fast as she ever had to chase down the taller girl. Her throat was burning, but she couldn't stop. It seemed to take forever to catch up with the girl, but when the Brazil player stopped for a split second to take aim, Shannon's foot belted the ball out of bounds.

Lynda mouthed a big *thank you* from the goal.

"All right!" Gregg yelled.

"Good move, Nelson!" Coach Reeder called to her.

The score was tied two-two at halftime. Shannon sipped from her water bottle as Coach Reeder discussed their game plan for the second half. She was desperately hoping she would get her second wind soon. The Brazil team was good, and she had been running ever since she saved the first goal.

"The other team wants to win this game just as much as you do," the coach told them. "They are in exactly the same situation. If they win today and tomorrow, they are guaranteed a spot in the championship game."

"Great," Samantha muttered.

The coach gave her an encouraging smile. "Don't get discouraged, girls. You can do it. We need a little more pressure on offense." He looked at Shannon. "And the defense should keep doing what it did in the first half."

The other team must have gotten the same pep talk at halftime, because they came roaring onto the field as if they were playing for the World Cup. Shannon saw the tall redhead coming toward her as soon as the game resumed. She hadn't played the first half; Shannon would have noticed her. The girl wasn't just tall, she had broader shoulders than half the boys at Hamilton High. Shannon refused to be intimidated. She wasn't going to let her team down simply because the other team had put an amazon on the field.

"Run up to the ball!" Gregg screamed from the sidelines. "Be aggressive."

Shannon nodded. There was no reason for her to wait for Big Red. She ran toward the girl, trying to keep her eye on the ball, but it was hard not to be distracted by the girl's size. Big Red took advantage of Shannon's split-second lapse and powered past her.

Luckily, Trish ran into the Brazil player's path and booted the ball back up the field.

"Thanks," Shannon said, breathing heavily.

"Just doing my part," Trish said with a grin.

Shannon smiled. She loved being part of the team. Ten days ago the Team Mexico girls had never seen each other; now they were a real team. It was a good feeling.

"Get ready, Nelson!" Gregg called when the ball began heading in her direction, but Samantha scooted around it and sent it flying back toward Brazil's goal.

For the first time, Shannon wasn't offended by Gregg's comments. The ball had been coming her way, and he wanted to be sure she saw it. Both Gregg and Coach Reeder seemed to want to win the game as much as the girls did.

"Oh, no, here she comes again," Trish said loudly.

Shannon saw the girl heading down her side of the field again, and she wondered if Big Red was choosing her side because she had made a mistake last time. Well, she was going to show the player that she wasn't afraid. When the girl ducked her head in concentration, Shannon gritted her teeth. She was going to be one roadblock that the redhead wouldn't forget. The Brazil player zigged to one side and Shannon matched her. As she dodged back to the other side, she suddenly felt her feet slipping.

The next thing she knew she was lying on her back on the hard ground. Her eyes were closed, but she could hear voices around her. And her head hurt as if she had been hit by a ten-ton truck.

Someone said, "Is she still unconscious?"

Unconscious? She'd been knocked out? Shannon opened one eye to see coaches from both teams leaning over her, with very worried expressions on their faces. To one side, she could see Trish and Franny wringing their hands in dismay. Lynda was blinking back tears. Shannon wanted to tell everyone not to worry, but when she tried to talk, her voice came out as one long moan.

"She's coming out of it," the Brazil coach said, sounding relieved. Shannon wondered lazily why he was so worried about her.

She tried to sit up, but Coach Reeder gently restrained her. "Don't move anything until we know you're all right. Do you know your name?"

Her mind was hazy, but she could answer that one. "I'm Shannon Nelson."

She didn't recognize her own voice. It sounded muffled and far away. The coach must have noticed the same thing. Slowly, he moved one hand toward her face. "How many fingers do you see?"

Shannon squinted at the slightly fuzzy image. "Three fingers."

He closed his hand and then flashed fingers in her face a second time. "How many do you see now?"

Had she been wrong the first time? Was this a test? Maybe he wanted her to be more specific. Shannon bit her lip and guessed, "Two fingers and one thumb?"

"She belongs in the infirmary," the other coach declared.

"As a precaution," Coach Reeder said, to Shannon's surprise. She had thought he would disagree because they obviously still needed her in the game.

"Are you sure you didn't hurt anything besides your head?"

"The rest of me is fine," Shannon answered. But actually, the rest of her was pretty sore.

Coach Reeder gathered her in his strong arms. Shannon rested her head on his shoulder, hoping it would hurt less if it didn't move with his every step. As they passed Gregg, the coach said, "Take over until I get back."

Shannon squinted at Gregg, half expecting him to criticize her for ruining the play. He didn't say anything as he stared at her. His lips were parted slightly, and his eyes looked dark with worry. It had to be her head injury. She was probably just imagining Gregg's concern. After all, they were in public. How could Assistant Coach Gregg Warner risk his image by worrying about her?

"Did you win?" she asked her teammates when they crowded around her infirmary bed two hours later.

"No. But we did our best to win it for you," Franny said.

"Without you on defense, we couldn't hold them," Samantha told her.

Shannon wanted to change the subject. The compliments made her uncomfortable. "Where did that redhead come from? Has anyone seen her before today?"

"Yeah," Trish said. "She spends most of the dinner hour in line . . . going back for third and fourth helpings!"

"Shannon, you need to eat more if you want to tackle people like her," Lynda added with a small smile.

"I didn't tackle her. She hit me." For the first time, Shannon wondered what had happened to the other girl. "Did she get hurt, too?"

"Not a chance." Franny rolled her eyes.

"That's probably a good thing," Trish said. "Otherwise she might be in the next room plotting revenge on you."

"That's your department," Shannon replied with a weak smile.

Lynda giggled.

"Ha, ha, ha," Trish said, unsuccessfully hiding a smile. "How long are they going to keep you here, anyway?"

"I have to stay overnight for observation. They don't think I have a concussion, but they want to be sure I'm okay," Shannon explained.

"Can you play tomorrow?" Trish wanted to know.

"It depends on what the doctor says in the morning."

"You have to be all right!" Samantha exclaimed.

"If you aren't playing, we won't have a chance," Lynda said in a sad voice.

"But you said we lost today." Shannon tried to sit up, but her head started to spin and she leaned back on her pillow. "I thought our team was out of the running for the championship."

"It depends on how a few other games turn out this afternoon," Trish explained. "If certain teams lose, then there's still a chance for us. But our odds will be a lot better if you're on the field tomorrow."

"I'll try," Shannon said. Maybe she would feel a lot better after a good night's sleep. Right now, she knew she wouldn't even be able to stand up on her own.

"Just take care of yourself." Lynda rested a hand on Shannon's arm. "You're more important than the championship. Right?" She looked around to the other girls.

"Sure," they chimed in.

"I bet Coach Reeder wouldn't say that," Shannon said, trying to lighten the mood.

"Are you kidding? He was a wreck when he came back to the field." Trish rolled her eyes. "I thought he and Gregg were going to have simultaneous heart attacks when you went down."

Lynda nodded in agreement. When the others turned to go, she gave Shannon a knowing glance that suggested Gregg had been visibly upset when she was hurt.

Was it possible? Did Gregg really care about her—or did he just want his team to win? She was going to have to consider the question . . . as soon as her head stopped spinning!

Chapter Twelve

Shannon could hear voices in the next room. The campus infirmary wasn't large, but there was at least one other camper being held captive—a camper who had a visitor.

She tried to imagine everyone back in the dorm. Lynda had called an hour ago to say Big Red had come to the dorm room to ask about her and to apologize. According to Lynda, the girl was very nice when she wasn't playing to win.

What was everyone doing now? Was Lynda calling her mother? Or was she in Franny's or Trish's room listening to the radio? Or maybe all of them were down in the living room watching reruns. Summer television was the worst.

Shannon wished she had brought her bear

Rosebud over to the infirmary. Maybe it was childish, but she could sure use a little company.

Her door opened slowly and Shannon didn't bother to look up. It was probably the nurse coming in for her hourly check. She regularly pushed back Shannon's eyelids to peer into her eyes, and then hushed Shannon so she could count her pulse.

"Are you awake?" someone whispered.

Shannon wondered if she was dreaming. The visitor sounded like Gregg. "I'm awake," she said, opening one eye.

"Good." He came up to the bed and Shannon asked herself how long a hallucination could last. The face above the huge bouquet of flowers even looked like Gregg's.

"Flowers? For me?"

"Not just flowers," he said with a grin. He set the arrangement on the table by her bed and then took a bag from behind the bouquet. "I heard the infirmary food is even worse than what we get in the dining hall. I thought you might need this."

"What?" She saw only daisies and chrysanthemums.

"This!" He handed her a take-out cup with the Mama's Kitchen logo on the front.

"Is this what I think it is?" Shannon asked, smiling broadly.

"The best chocolate malt in town." He dug into his pocket and offered her a straw.

"You thought of everything." Shannon hadn't the faintest idea why he had done all this for her, but she was impressed.

"It's no big deal. I just thought you might need a straw in case you couldn't sit up."

"I sat up to eat the goulash they handed out at dinner time, and it didn't bother me too much—until I tasted it." She tried to sit up and fluff her pillow without spilling her malt.

"Let me help," he insisted. Gregg leaned over and folded her soft pillow in half, then wedged it behind her back for support.

"Thanks." She slipped the paper cover off the straw and slid it through the small hole in the plastic lid. The rich, chocolaty liquid felt cool and refreshing against her parched throat. "This is sure thick," she said after she swallowed.

"I knew you'd love Mama's malts," Gregg said.

"I'm not sure Nurse Frankenstein would appreciate this late-night treat, though," Shannon joked. "I'm sure something so yummy is against the rules."

"Speaking of Frankenstein," Gregg began in a serious tone, "I'm very sorry about what happened to you today."

Shannon smiled. "She was rather large, wasn't she?"

"I think you might have had a better chance running into a tank," he told her.

She gently rubbed the lump on top of her head. "I just can't believe she wasn't hurt at all."

"If it helps, the ref kicked her out of the game."

"Why?" Shannon asked. "We just ran into each other. She didn't mean to hurt me."

"I guess the ref didn't see it that way. Neither did I." Gregg pulled up the chair beside her bed and sat down. "I felt terrible when I saw you lying on the field."

"I suppose I didn't look too terrific when I was lying there out cold."

"Shannon, I wish you wouldn't make jokes about today. I was really worried about you," Gregg said softly.

She held the cold malt in both hands and slowly turned her head toward Gregg. "I don't understand what's been going on today. Some of the team stopped by after the game, and they were upset when I said I didn't know if I could play tomorrow. They acted as if they couldn't win without me. And now you're being incredibly nice. Is this Be Kind to Shannon Nelson Day, or what?"

Gregg frowned. "I don't know why you say stuff like that. You know, it was my fault you got hurt today."

Shannon blinked in surprise. "*Your* fault? Did you pay that girl to attack me?" When he shook his head, she said, "I didn't think so. What's this all about?"

"I've been pretty hard on you this session."

Shannon couldn't help adding, "Especially this week."

"I suppose that's true. Do you know why I pushed you so hard?"

"Of course. You wanted to show all your counselor buddies that there was nothing special between you and one of your lowly campers."

He stared at her. "What are you talking about?"

Maybe he didn't want to admit what he had done, but she wasn't about to back down. "I know you were embarrassed when Trish turned on the lights last Friday night. So you had to find ways to prove I was just another camper."

Gregg Warner actually blushed. "Maybe . . . I guess I did overdo things for a few days. I

144

wasn't very nice to you at Campers Night Out or the waterslide. I'm sorry."

"What about that stupid contest?" If he was going to start being sorry, she wanted an apology for Monday.

Gregg grinned crookedly. "The one-on-one was a contest and nothing more. I would have given those stinky socks to whoever got the lowest score."

"Even Trish?"

He nodded. "I would have given them to Trish if she earned them, although she would have thrown them back in my face."

"You're a brave man to risk Trish's temper," Shannon joked.

"I'd rather have Trish mad at me than to have you think those terrible things about me," he said gravely.

Shannon was confused. She had been so sure she understood his motives. Trying to sort out these new ideas was making her head hurt. She took a sip of her drink and stalled for time, hoping for some inspiration. She had no idea how to respond to his admission.

He rested his elbows on his knees and leaned closer to her. "I've been hard on you at practice because you have no idea how good you could be. Somehow, you seem to know where the ball will be before it gets there . . . but then you put your head down instead of watching."

"Is that what happened today? Is that why I was hit?" Shannon asked.

"I don't know exactly what happened today. It's all a blur in my mind," he admitted.

"Mine, too," Shannon said with a faint smile.

"You're missing my point," he told her. "I kept yelling at you to run faster and work harder because you could improve your skills. You're already very good, but it wouldn't take much for you to be even better."

"Are you telling me I could get a starting spot on my school team this fall?"

Gregg groaned. "Oh no, I've been helping Jefferson High's biggest competitor! They'll probably shoot me when I get back home."

"Don't make jokes! Do you really think I'm varsity starting material?" Shannon persisted.

He nodded. "But I don't want to talk about the Jefferson-Hamilton rivalry. I'd like to talk about . . . us."

Shannon choked a little on her malt. Us? Had he said the word "us"?

"I've made a lot of mistakes, but I had reasons. And not the ones you think I had," he told her.

"So. Prove me wrong," she challenged.

Gregg swallowed hard. "It was a major deal for me to be an assistant coach here this year, and I really wanted to do everything right. When I saw you at the first practice, I knew you could be a great player if someone just made you work harder. Well, my interest gave you a concussion today."

"The doctor doesn't think I have a concussion." Shannon thought the news would make him happy, but he still frowned.

"But you could have. I kept screaming at you to be aggressive, until I forced you to throw your body in front of someone three times your weight."

"I didn't do that because you were screaming at me," she said. "I did it for the team so we could play in the championship on Saturday."

He shrugged his shoulders and Shannon knew he wasn't convinced. If he truly wanted to blame himself, she couldn't do much about it. Besides, she was more interested in what he had to say about them. "Uh—what were you saying before about . . . us?"

Gregg started tracing patterns on her blanket with one finger. "I was explaining how important it was for me to do my job right. I thought I shouldn't like you because I'm a coach, and you're a camper. I didn't want that to keep me from being fair on the job."

"I—I guess I can understand your feelings." Although she wished he hadn't avoided her so completely, she had seen coaches play favorites before. A whole team could get mad if that kind of thing happened.

"Logic doesn't have much to do with reality," he said after a moment. "What I mean is, knowing the facts didn't keep me from caring about you. I couldn't stop my feelings."

"Really?" Shannon was suddenly light-headed, and she knew it had nothing to do with her game injury. Gregg Warner was saying he cared about her!

"Really." He managed to keep a serious face when he added, "And what are you going to do about it?"

Shannon slowly leaned forward, making sure her head wasn't going to start pounding again. Gregg seemed to know exactly what she had in mind and stretched toward her.

Their lips barely brushed against each other's. Shannon inched closer to him, and then she thought she heard something. She jerked away from Gregg and looked across the room at the light switch.

He laughed and asked, "Were you checking for Trish?"

Shannon blushed. "You bet I was!"

Gregg took the chocolate malt out of Shannon's hands and set it on the bedside table. "Just in case Trish is on her way over here, let's not waste any time. I think you owe me a real kiss."

"*I* owe *you*? Who was the one who stopped kissing me when—"

Gregg slipped one arm around her back and carefully pulled her closer until their lips met. For a second, Shannon was amazed by his gentle touch. It was clear he didn't want to hurt her. Then her brain stopped working. She'd had problems keeping her thoughts together before Gregg came into her room, but now they were scattered in all directions.

Her head was still spinning when he suddenly stopped kissing her. "What's wrong?"

"Someone just opened your door."

"Not Trish," Shannon whispered against his lips.

"Excuse me, young man," a woman said, too loudly. "Visiting hours are over!"

Shannon closed her eyes. "Don't tell me— it's Nurse Frankenstein."

Gregg smiled at her and pressed a soft kiss against her forehead before he stood up. "I'll see you tomorrow, Shannon."

"Yeah—I'll see you." Her voice was so soft she didn't recognize it.

The nurse cleared her throat at the door. "Young man."

"Yes, ma'am," Gregg said, turning to face her. "I'm on my way."

Nurse Jones waited in the doorway until he had marched past her. But before she could shut the door and chase him into the hall, he peeked back over his shoulder once more. "Sleep well!" he whispered.

Sleep? Shannon didn't know if she would sleep again for a week. What if she woke up in the morning and found out this was all a dream? What if she had been unconscious ever since the game, and all this was happening in her sleeping brain?

Shannon pinched herself, and then reached for the cup on the bedside table. If there really was a Mama's Kitchen chocolate malt in it, then she would have to believe Gregg had been in her room. She took a long sip and savored the chocolate taste. Yes! Gregg Warner had said he liked her. And he had kissed her!

When she fell back on her pillow, her head was sore. But at least it wasn't pounding like it had been when they first brought her to the infirmary. And it wasn't spinning the way it had been when Gregg had kissed her. She was just tired. Too much had happened for one day!

She had been knocked out on the soccer field and kissed by the only boy she really cared about in the whole camp. Shannon giggled. She knew just what her mother would think. She would say it had been a rather extreme way to get a boy's attention.

But Gregg had noticed her before she collapsed today. He had thought she was a good soccer player who could be even better. And then he had started to like her, even when she ruined his image as the perfect assistant coach. Shannon wasn't sure if she wanted to fall asleep. Her dreams couldn't be any better than what had just happened to her.

Chapter Thirteen

"Where would you like to sit?"

"Anywhere," Shannon told Greg as he balanced a lunch tray in each hand. She wanted to tell him that he didn't need to treat her like an invalid, but it was fun having him take such good care of her.

Although the doctor had said she couldn't practice or play in a game that day, he had assured her that she was all right. Even her parents were convinced she was fine, after both she and the doctor talked to her father that morning. Of course, her mother was going to fuss over her when she got home in three days, but that would be fairly normal.

"Will it bother you if the sun is in your eyes?" Gregg asked.

Shannon shook her head. After almost two

weeks of being harassed by the guy, all the loving attention was mind-boggling. "The only thing that will bother me is starvation."

"Right." He stopped at the next table with two empty chairs. He carefully placed the tray with her lunch on it—tuna and fresh vegetables and dip—in front of a chair. "Can you manage okay?"

Suppressing a smile, Shannon nodded and sat down in her seat. People were staring at her. Did the whole camp know what had happened? Or was everyone amazed to see Gregg openly spending time with her?

"Are you sure you're all right? Could I get you more food?" he inquired as he sat down.

"I'm fine," she told him, putting her hand on his. "Please relax."

He turned his hand over beneath hers and wrapped his fingers around her hand. "I can't help thinking I should have faced my feelings and been honest with you sooner—"

Steve slapped Gregg on the shoulder. "Warner, we need you at the back table. Coaching session."

Gregg shifted uneasily in his seat. "I'm not sure I should—"

"Go ahead," Shannon interrupted, taking a bite of her carrot stick.

"You'll be all right?" Gregg seemed nervous about leaving her alone.

"Yes." She picked up her tray. "I'm going to find my friends. I'll see you at the game. We can hang out together on the sidelines, okay?"

Gregg smiled. At last he seemed to believe she wasn't going to get angry with him if he left her. "That's right, we'll be working together. Although I'd rather see you on the field, I won't mind your company."

"Well, if you don't hurry to your meeting, the games will start late. Do you want everyone to blame you when the games end so late that we miss the second half of *Love's Destiny*?"

He slapped his forehead. "I don't want to think about what the girls would do to me if they missed that soap. I'll see you later."

To her amazement, he kissed her on the cheek before he headed for the back of the dining hall. When Shannon walked over and sat down beside Lynda at her team's table, she discovered that all the girls had been watching her and Gregg.

"If I get knocked out in today's game, will I get a guy?" Trish joked.

"Don't even think about it!" Lynda scolded. "It's bad enough Shannon can't play until tomorrow."

"Well, be optimistic," Trish said cheerfully. "If Japan, Peru, and Holland lose today . . . we still might be in the championship tomorrow."

"Fat chance," Samantha grumbled. "The Cayman Islands aren't going to beat Holland. What decent team would be named after a resort."

"She's probably right," Franny told Trish softly. "We might not get a chance to win the big one."

"I'm sorry." Everyone stared at Shannon in surprise. "I mean, I don't know if we would have won yesterday if I stayed in the game, but it sure didn't help when they had to carry me off the field."

"It wasn't your fault," Lynda pointed out, and the others nodded in agreement.

"If anyone should apologize, it should be Big Red!" Trish's tone invited no further discussion.

"I bet your head barely hurt at all after Gregg stopped by," Samantha said with a smile.

Trish got a wicked grin on her face. "Did he kiss you and make it all better?"

"Give me a break." Shannon waved a celery stick at her teammates. "Is this any way to treat an injured person? Someone who almost gave her life for the team?"

Lynda threw her arm around Shannon. "I'm so glad to hear you making jokes. Now I know you're fine!"

"I think it's time for us to get dressed for the game." Although Trish still had some spaghetti left on her plate, she picked up her tray and the others followed her lead.

They were talking and laughing as they walked toward the conveyor belt at the back of the dining hall. Suddenly Shannon saw a pool of milk on the floor. "Trish, watch out!" she yelled.

The warning came too late. Trish stepped right into the spill and her foot slid forward. When she jerked back to catch her balance, everything flew off her tray.

The spaghetti noodles and sauce shot off the plate and soared across the coaches' table. As the plate and cutlery hit the floor with a crash, Shannon held her breath, wondering where the slop would land. Gregg quickly leaned out of the way and the spaghetti hit the guy next to him, staining his white shirt with a puddle of red tomato sauce.

Trish seemed frozen in time. She was still holding her empty tray. Her green eyes were huge as she watched the spaghetti sauce drip down the guy's shirt. "I'm *so* sorry," she said.

"Let's get out of here," Samantha whispered.

They scrambled out of the dining hall in record time; but before she left, Shannon saw Gregg wink at her. He had been right about Trish. Life around her was never dull.

Trish collapsed against the wall outside and pressed her hand to her forehead. "I can't believe I did that."

"At least it was a young guy," Franny said. "He's probably just some assistant coach."

"What do you mean, *just* an assistant coach?" Shannon inquired with a mock scowl.

Franny giggled. "I think I mean Trish was very lucky her lunch didn't land on Gregg. Shannon would have killed her!"

"I can't believe he's our referee!" Trish wailed when the spaghetti-splattered guy walked onto the field after lunch. He had changed his shirt, but everyone knew he was the same guy by the way he glared at Trish.

Lynda whistled. "I hope this isn't some kind of omen."

Before the game started, Gregg handed Shannon his Detroit Tigers baseball cap. "You should keep the sun out of your eyes," he said.

Shannon was touched. Smiling, she tugged

the cap down to her ears until she could no longer see the soccer field.

"That's not how to wear it." Grinning, he flicked the cap back on her head.

Once the game started, Shannon felt awkward. She tapped Gregg on the arm. "This is so strange. I haven't watched my team from the sidelines since seventh grade."

"How does it feel?"

She gritted her teeth when the girl playing her position let a ball speed past her. "Frustrating."

"I bet it is," he said with sympathy.

Lynda caught the ball before it could sail into the goal for a score. Shannon clapped and shouted in delight.

Although the team was doing all right without her, it just didn't seem fair to Shannon. After her friends and Gregg had helped her realize she was a better soccer player than she was letting herself believe, she wanted to get out on the field and try out her new confidence. If she had played decently when she thought she was bad, it made sense to Shannon that she could really be good now that she had more faith in herself.

"Please let us win," she whispered.

"The game isn't going so badly that we need prayers . . . yet," Gregg told her with a smile.

158

Shannon's cheeks grew warm when she realized he had overheard her plea. She wanted the team to win so she could play in the championship game the next day! If they lost today, they had no hope for the championship. She just had to play one last time.

"Watch out!" Gregg called to Lynda, but the ball skidded under her outstretched arm and into the net.

Lynda stood up and shook her head. Shannon knew how bad her roommate felt about letting the other team get the first point.

"It's okay," Coach Reeder told her. "It's just the first quarter. We still have plenty of soccer to play."

The coach's words echoed in Shannon's mind as the Mexico players trudged off the field an hour later. Although they had had plenty of time to come back in the game after that first goal, things had gotten progressively worse.

"Eight to one," Samantha groaned as she grabbed a juice box from the cooler.

"At least when we lose, we lose big," Trish said, making Shannon wonder if anything really got her down. The girl seemed capable of joking about everything.

"Tomorrow we can go to the championship

159

game and watch how soccer is *supposed* to be played," Lynda said glumly.

"Ladies," Coach Reeder interrupted, "some days you have it and some days you don't. You didn't play a bad game out there, but the other team didn't make a single mistake."

"Such as . . . getting knocked out the other day." Shannon couldn't help but feel partially responsible for the loss.

"Or spilling lunch on the referee," Trish said with a crooked smile.

"We don't need excuses, and we don't need to assign blame." The coach's stern gaze moved from one girl to another. "Each of you has learned a lot, and you have improved immensely as a team since your first game. Be proud of what you have accomplished."

"He's right," Gregg said as he put one arm around Shannon and the other around Trish. "It's been a lot of fun working with all of you."

"But some of us were more fun than others, right?" Trish teased, glancing over at Shannon.

Gregg hung his head as if he'd been caught misbehaving. "You're right, Trish. It's been *real* special working with you!"

The girls burst out laughing.

Out of the corner of her eye, Shannon saw

Deb Smith approaching. She assumed the other girl would simply pass by without saying hello, but she was wrong.

"Laugh now, cry later," Deb said to Shannon and the rest of her team.

"What's your problem? Can't you stand to see someone happy?" Trish asked. Apparently, she had also seen more than enough of Deb in the past two weeks.

"I just wanted to say we'll be playing you in tomorrow's consolation game," Deb answered.

"You mean Denmark lost today?" Trish inquired with a smirk.

"Not as badly as *your* team managed to lose. I'm sure we all know how things will turn out tomorrow!" she said confidently as she stalked off the field toward the dormitory.

"Does she eat lemons for breakfast every morning, or what?" Gregg asked. "I mean, she's unpleasant all the time . . . even when she's trying to be friendly."

Shannon knew Deb wasn't quite as bad as everyone was thinking. "Deb hates to lose," she explained. "In fact, I'm not sure she ever learned how to lose gracefully."

"That's kind of sad," Franny said. "Not that we all should be experts at losing, but it happens to everyone once in a while."

"Let's hope it's not us tomorrow," Lynda said, frowning.

"We beat them in our first game," Samantha reminded everyone.

"I don't know," Franny said thoughtfully. She didn't seem to share Samantha's optimism. "I saw part of a Denmark game yesterday, and Deb is really hot. If you remember, she got thrown out of our game early on."

Shannon and Gregg shared a smile. "She's right," Shannon told them. "We can talk about Deb's attitude, but she's a great player. When she's concentrating on the game, no one can stop her."

"I bet you can," Trish insisted.

"Really!" Lynda's eyes sparkled with excitement. "You know her from your high school team. You've seen all her tricks."

"Let's go someplace where you can tell us everything you know about her style," Trish suggested.

"And I thought you were going to need me to lift your spirits and tell you not to worry about the game!" Gregg shook his head. "You don't need me at all."

"That's not quite true," Shannon whispered to him.

"Shannon, are you ready to help us come

up with a winning strategy?" Trish seemed determined to beat Deb's team.

"You bet! Will I see you later?" Shannon whispered to Gregg.

"Definitely! I'll call you before dinner," he said to her privately. Then he turned to the team. "Do whatever you have to do—short of knocking Deb out cold—" Gregg elbowed Shannon and everyone laughed—"and I'll be there tomorrow to see you teach Denmark how to play soccer!"

Everyone clapped and pulled Gregg into a team huddle. "One-two-three, go Mexico!" they screamed. Shannon hoped Deb and her team-mates could hear them all the way across campus.

Chapter Fourteen

"We're going to win! We're going to win!"

The chanting grew louder and more spirited as the Mexico team walked to the field Saturday morning. Trish wanted to intimidate the Denmark team before the referee blew the whistle to start the game. Shannon wasn't sure if it would work, but it was certainly bolstering their spirits.

A few of the girls on the other team looked up and stared at them. Shannon might have been embarrassed if she weren't surrounded by a dozen other yellow-shirted girls yelling along with her. When a few Denmark girls started to giggle, Trish raised her eyebrows. There was no mistaking the expression on her face. It said: *Aren't we going to surprise them?*

Samantha amazed them on the first play of the game. She commanded the kickoff and bullied the ball down the field and promptly slammed it into the goal. Shannon was stunned. Although Samantha was a good forward, she had never pushed her way down the field so aggressively before.

When Denmark got the ball, no one was surprised that it was passed right to Deb. She danced around the Mexico players until she made it down to Shannon's part of the field. Remembering Gregg's advice, Shannon ignored Deb's footwork and focused on the ball instead. The second Deb jogged to her left, Shannon's foot darted forward and booted the ball back to her own forwards.

"Go, Samantha!" Shannon yelled when the other girl stopped the flying ball with her head and then began dribbling toward the Denmark goal.

By the second half, the Denmark girls weren't passing the ball to Deb anymore. It didn't matter to Shannon. With Gregg smiling encouragement at her, she stopped anyone who dared get close to Lynda's goal area. Shannon felt a heady exhilaration. She had never played so well before.

As they walked off the field between the third and fourth quarters, Shannon overheard someone on the other team saying, "I thought she was supposed to be hurt."

Another girl laughed. "If that's what a shot in the head can do for a person, I'm going to see if Bertha will hit me."

Bertha? Big Red's real name was Bertha? Shannon couldn't think of anything more appropriate. Someday she would have to thank Big Bertha for changing her life.

"What can I say?" Coach Reeder asked as the girls crowded around him. "We're ahead five to zero. Just keep doing what you've been doing."

Time seemed to fly in the last quarter. Shannon was startled when the final whistle blew. They had done it! They had taken third place in the camp tournament!

She joined her teammates running and jumping as they left the field for the last time.

Lynda threw out her arms and captured Shannon in a bear hug. "You did it!"

"I did it? You were part of the team out there," Shannon reminded her roommate.

"The ball never came near me, thanks to you. I'm just glad it's the last game—Coach Reeder would probably send me home, because this team doesn't need a goalie with you around!"

166

"Fat chance. I just had a good game," Shannon argued.

"Don't start making excuses for yourself," Gregg advised, coming up behind them. "You played a good game because you're a good player."

"But today *was* special," she told him. Shannon couldn't begin to list all the reasons the game had been different for her. It was the first one since she had started to trust her own potential as a player. It was the first one since she discovered Gregg liked her. And she hadn't done it alone: her whole team was dynamite!

"Time to shake hands," Coach Reeder reminded the girls before they scattered for their victory celebration.

The Mexico girls lined up and met the Denmark team in the center of the field. As they filed past each other, they shook hands. Shannon was a little nervous when it was her turn to meet Deb.

"Good game, Nelson," Deb said as their hands met. She smiled at Shannon. "I'm sure glad we're on the same team at home."

Shannon glanced around her. What if Deb had finally been nice to her and no one else had heard it?

"Congratulations," Lynda said as they fin-

167

ished going through the line. Shannon thought she was still talking about the game until she added, "I didn't think Deb would ever be civil to you."

Trish came over and slapped Shannon on the shoulder. "Nice going. Your high school team should be undefeatable with both you and Deb. If the two of you actually start talking and working together . . . watch out!"

It was an interesting concept, Shannon thought. It had been fun being part of a team with Lynda and Trish and the others. Would it be possible for her to feel the same way on the Hamilton High team? She hoped so—it was a great feeling!

Gregg grabbed her by the arms when she came off the field. He had a wide smile on his face when he told her, "Good game. You are one hot soccer lady."

"Hot on the field or off?" she teased.

"Both." He bent his head toward her and slid his arms around her waist. Shannon's arms automatically slipped around his neck.

She knew he was going to kiss her, but she couldn't believe he would do it with so many people around them. "What about Trish and the others?" she teased.

He kept smiling. "I don't care. Do you?"

Shannon shook her head with a sigh and

met his lips in a kiss. She was so crazy about Gregg Warner that she didn't care if the whole world knew!

She hugged Gregg closer, still unable to believe her good luck. This camp had been so much more than she had hoped for. She'd not only improved her soccer skills—she had gained a whole new confidence in herself. She'd met a terrific group of girls, and . . . Shannon looked up at Gregg and smiled.

"Penny for your thoughts?" he asked, brushing a strand of hair from her face. Slightly embarrassed, Shannon shrugged. "Well, I'll tell you what I was thinking," Gregg continued with a happy smile. "I just can't believe that we're both from the same town. It's so perfect. Soccer camp may be ending, but—" He tightened his arms around her waist. "We're just beginning."

We hope you enjoyed reading this book. If you would like to receive further information about available titles in the Bantam series, just write to the address below, with your name and address: Kim Prior, Bantam Books, 61-63 Uxbridge Road, Ealing, London W5 5SA.

If you live in Australia or New Zealand and would like more information about the series, please write to:

Sally Porter
Transworld Publishers
(Australia) Pty Ltd
15-23 Helles Avenue
Moorebank
NSW 2170
AUSTRALIA

Kiri Martin
Transworld Publishers (NZ) Ltd
Cnr. Moselle and Waipareira
Avenues
Henderson
Auckland
NEW ZEALAND

All Bantam and Young Adult books are available at your bookshop or newsagent, or can be ordered at the following address: Corgi/ Bantam Books, Cash Sales Department, PO Box 11, Falmouth, Cornwall, TR10 9EN.

Please list the title(s) you would like, and send together with a cheque or postal order. You should allow for the cost of book(s) plus postage and packing charges as follows:
80p for one book
£1.00 for two books
£1.20 for three books
£1.40 for four books
Five or more books free.

Please note that payment must be made in pounds sterling; other currencies are unacceptable.

(The above applies to readers in the UK and Republic of Ireland only)

BFPO customers, please allow for the cost of the book(s) plus the following for postage and packing: 80p for the first book, and 20p per copy for each additional book.

Overseas customers, please allow £1.50 for postage and packing for the first book, £1.00 for the second book, and 30p for each subsequent title ordered.